ILLUMINATION PRESENTS

THE SECRET LIFE OF PETS

STÉPHANE LAPUSS'

GOUM

# PET TAILS

SECRET LIFE OF PETS

JUNE 2019. Published by Titan Comics, a division of Titan Publishing Group, Ltd. 144 Southwark Street, London SE1 0UP. Titan Comics is a registered tradedmark of Titan Publishing Group, Ltd. All rights reserved.© 2019 - The Secret Life of Pets is a trademark and copyright of Universal Studios. © 2019 Universal City Studios LLC. All Rights Reserved. TCN 3549. A CIP catalogue record for this title is available from the British Library.

PRINTED IN CHINA
10 9 8 7 6 5 4 3 2 1

ISBN: 9781787733145

ILLUMINATION PRESENTS

THE SECRET LIFE OF

**PETs**

**PET TAILS**

# WRITTEN BY:
# STÉPHANE LAPUSS'

# ART BY:
# GOUM

## ENGLISH TRANSLATION:
## MONTANA KANE

THE SECRET LIFE OF PETS

# ROLL-CALL

WHO'S WHO IN THE SECRET LIFE OF PETS

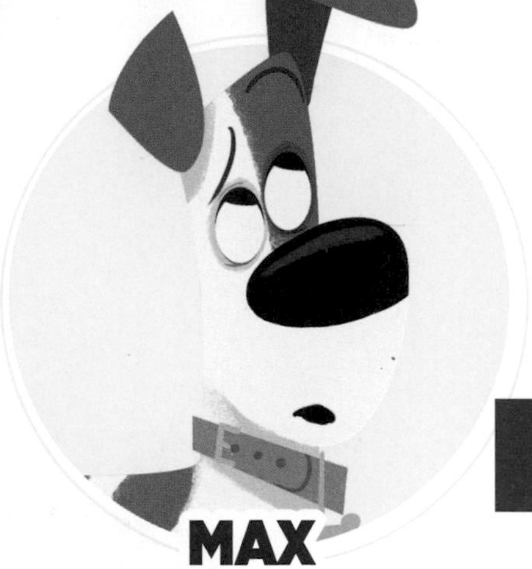

## MAX

Neurotic, pampered terrier mix.

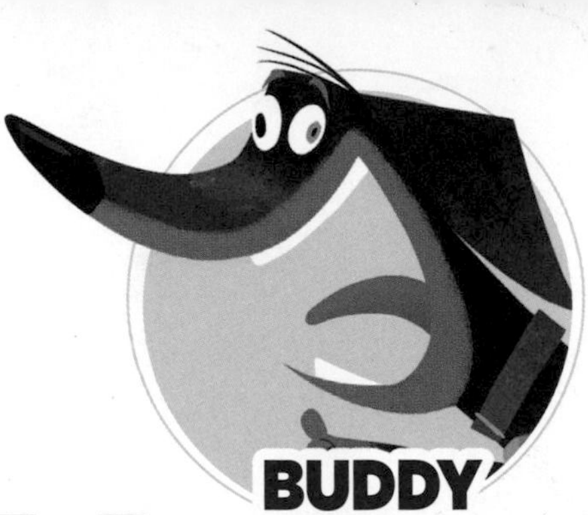

## BUDDY

Sarcastic Dachshund.
Short. Long.
Awesome.

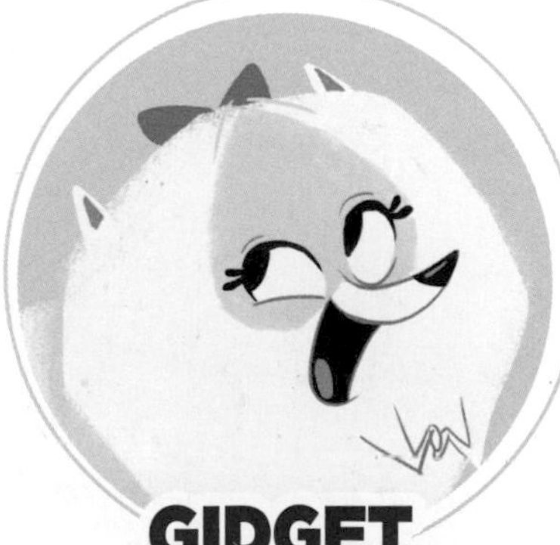

## GIDGET

A Naive, but gutsy Pomeranian.
50% fluff, 110% tough.
Gutsy & perfect.

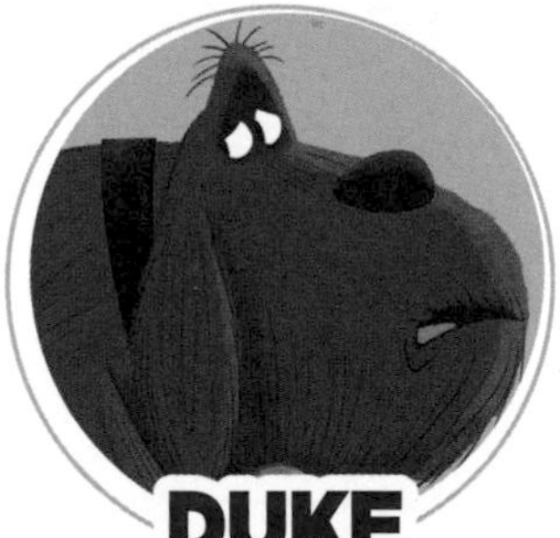

## DUKE

Big hairy dog.

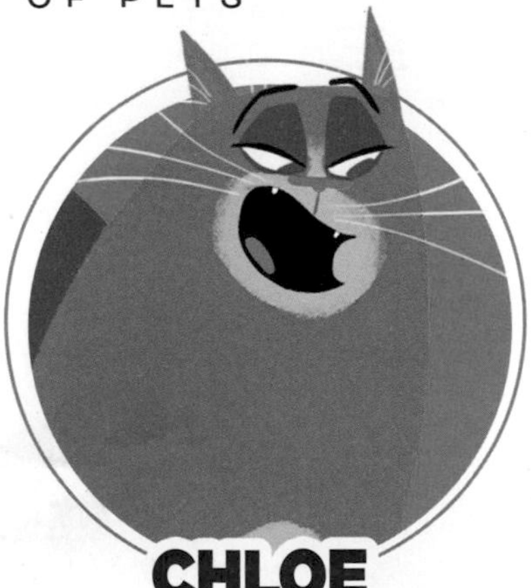

## CHLOE

Superior... in every way.

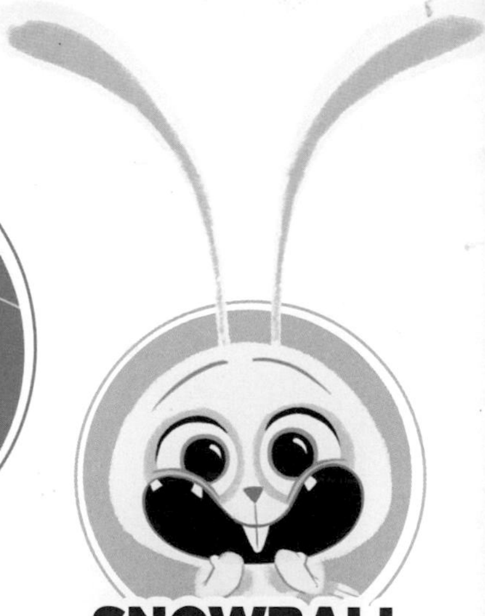

## SNOWBALL

White fluffy rabbit.
Insanely cute.
Also, insane.

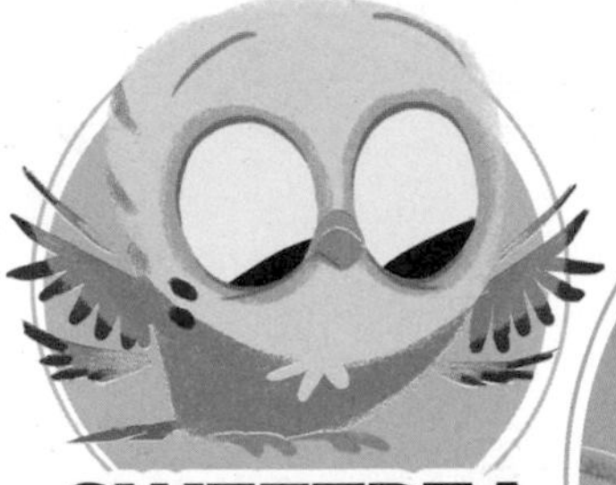

## SWEETPEA

Fearless Budgie.

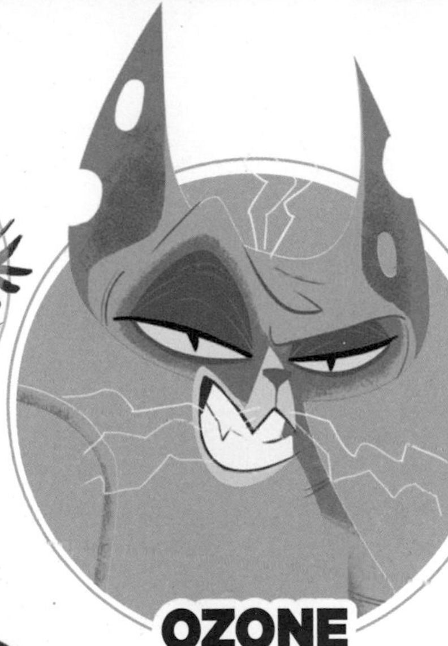

## OZONE

Hairless alley cat, ugly inside and out.

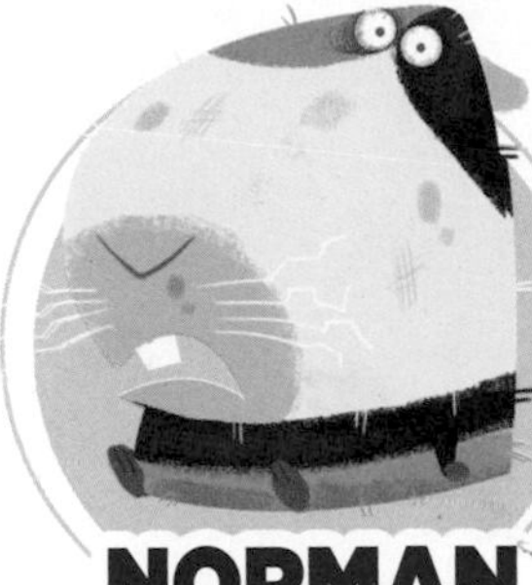

## NORMAN

Guinea pig with the brain the size of a pea, which he chooses to use only half of.

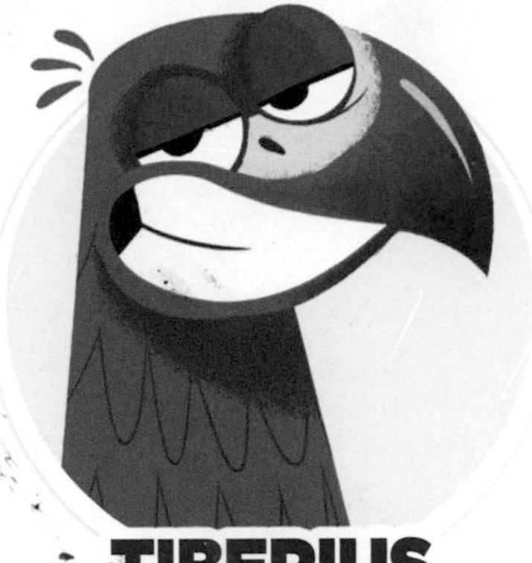

## TIBERIUS

Red-tailed hawk.

Sharp wit, even sharper talons.

# SUPPORTING CHARACTERS

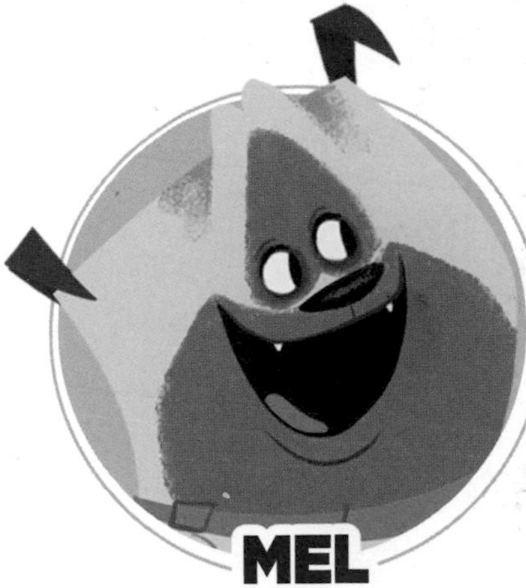

## MEL

Optimistic and extremely excitable Pug.

Lady-killer on the inside, dopey Pug on the outside.

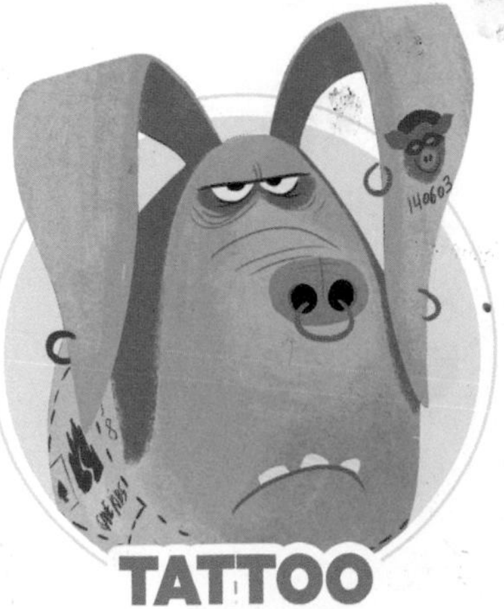

## TATTOO

Pot-bellied pig

Art Lover

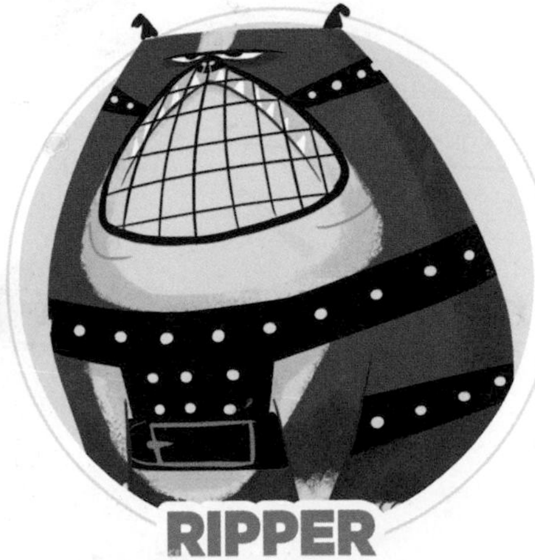

## RIPPER

Bulldog. No Bark, just bite.

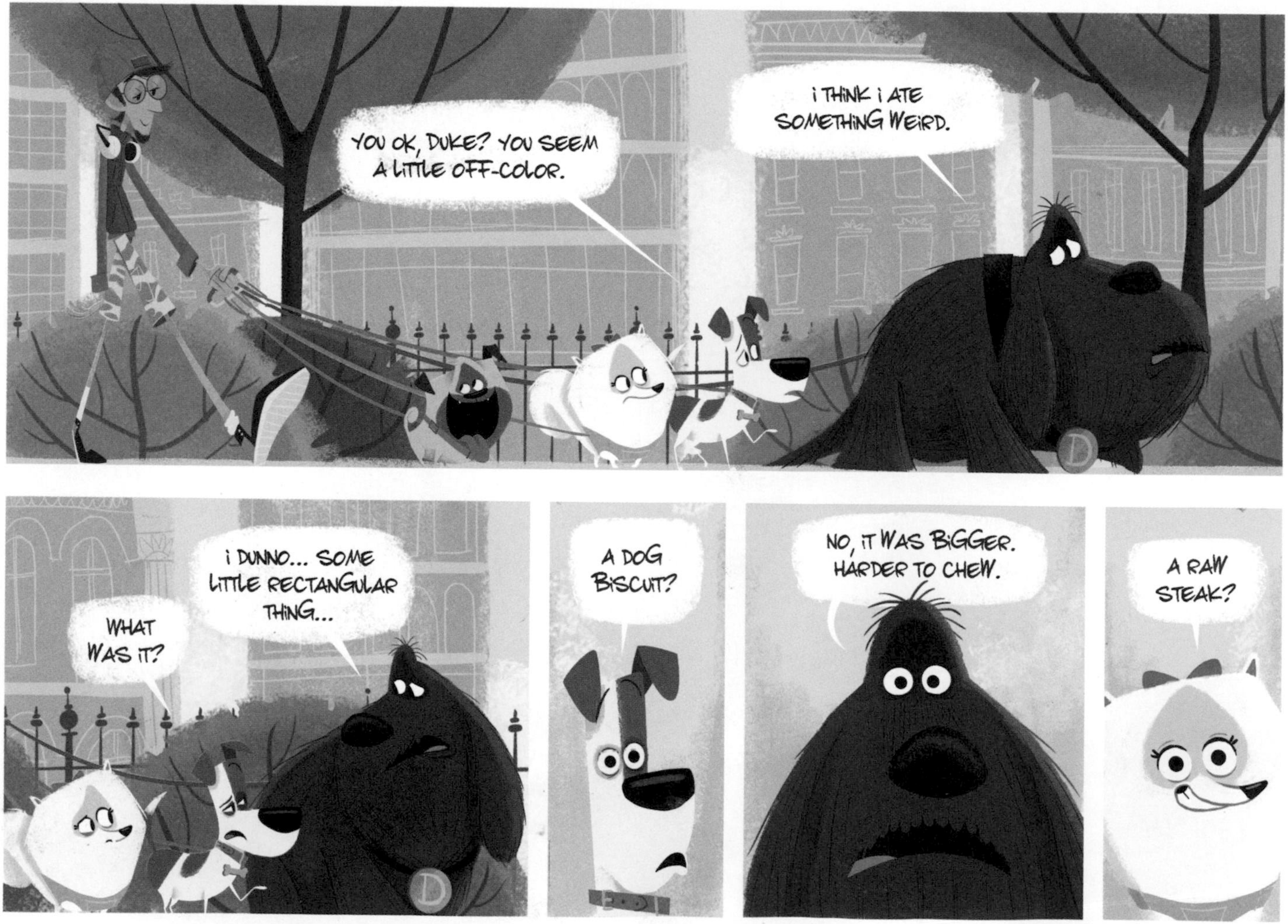
YOU OK, DUKE? YOU SEEM A LITTLE OFF-COLOR.
I THINK I ATE SOMETHING WEIRD.
WHAT WAS IT?
I DUNNO... SOME LITTLE RECTANGULAR THING...
A DOG BISCUIT?
NO, IT WAS BIGGER. HARDER TO CHEW.
A RAW STEAK?

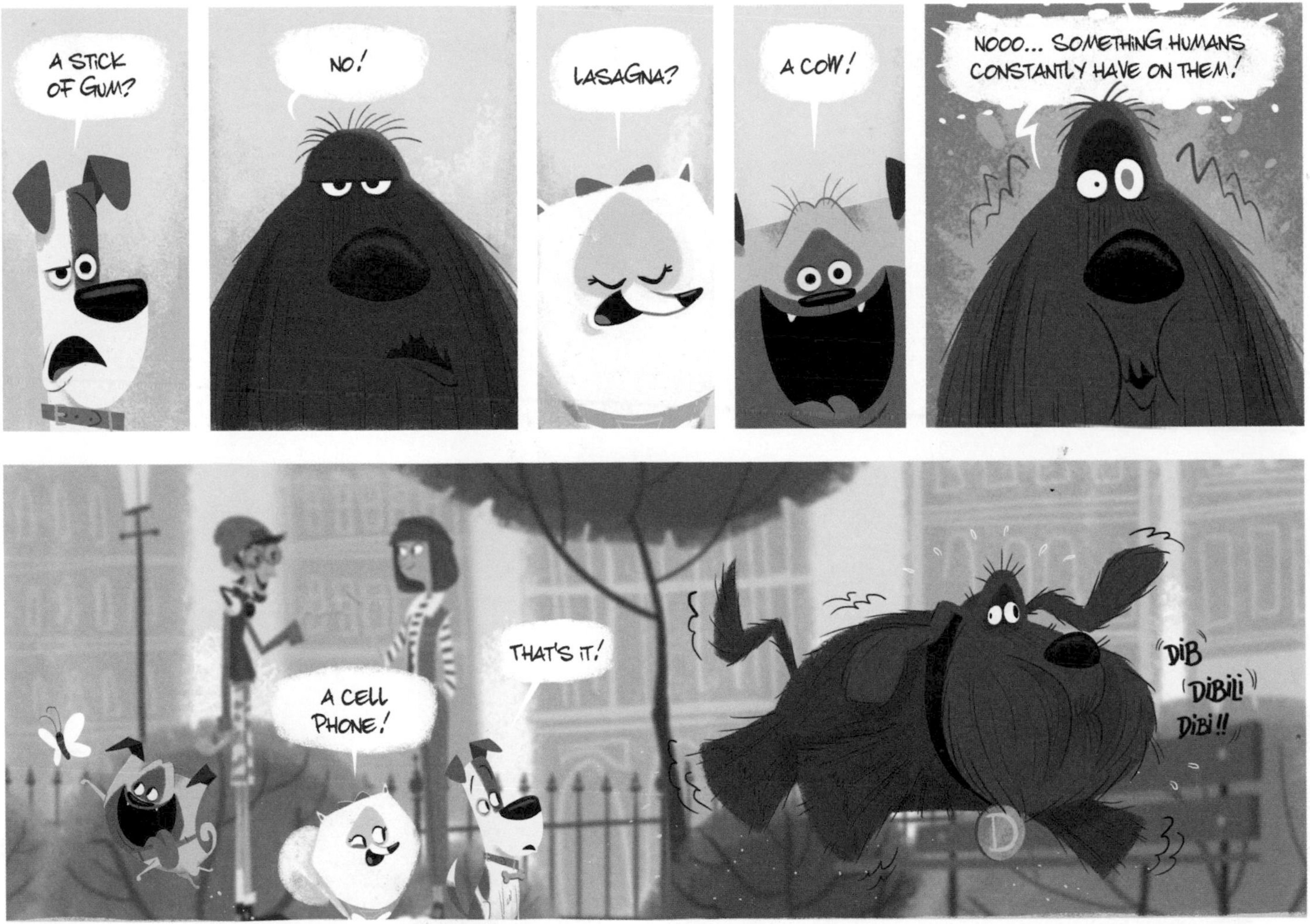
A STICK OF GUM?
NO!
LASAGNA?
A COW!
NOOO... SOMETHING HUMANS CONSTANTLY HAVE ON THEM!
A CELL PHONE!
THAT'S IT!
DIB DIBILI DIBI!!

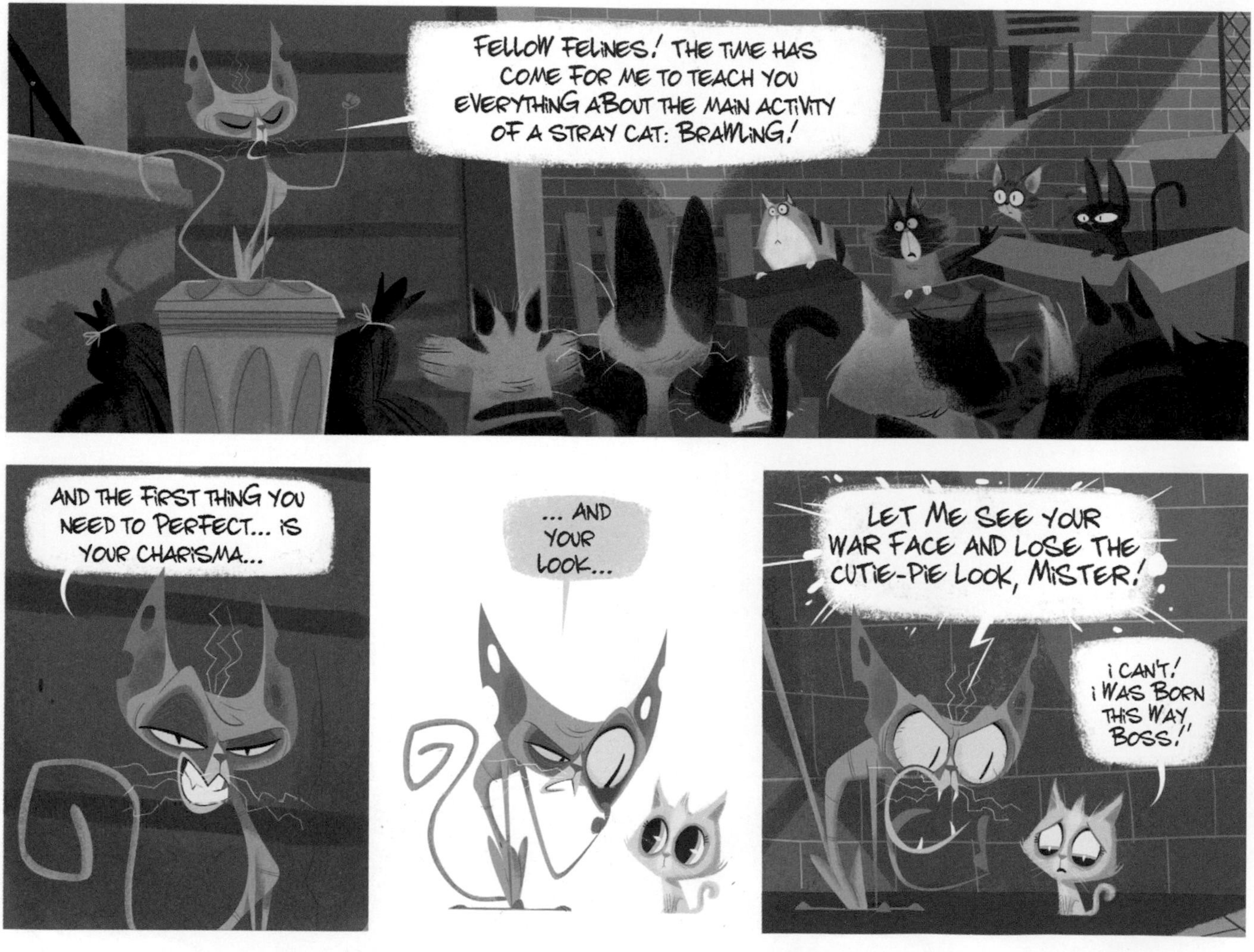
FELLOW FELINES! THE TIME HAS COME FOR ME TO TEACH YOU EVERYTHING ABOUT THE MAIN ACTIVITY OF A STRAY CAT: BRAWLING!
AND THE FIRST THING YOU NEED TO PERFECT... IS YOUR CHARISMA...
... AND YOUR LOOK...
LET ME SEE YOUR WAR FACE AND LOSE THE CUTIE-PIE LOOK, MISTER!
I CAN'T! I WAS BORN THIS WAY, BOSS!

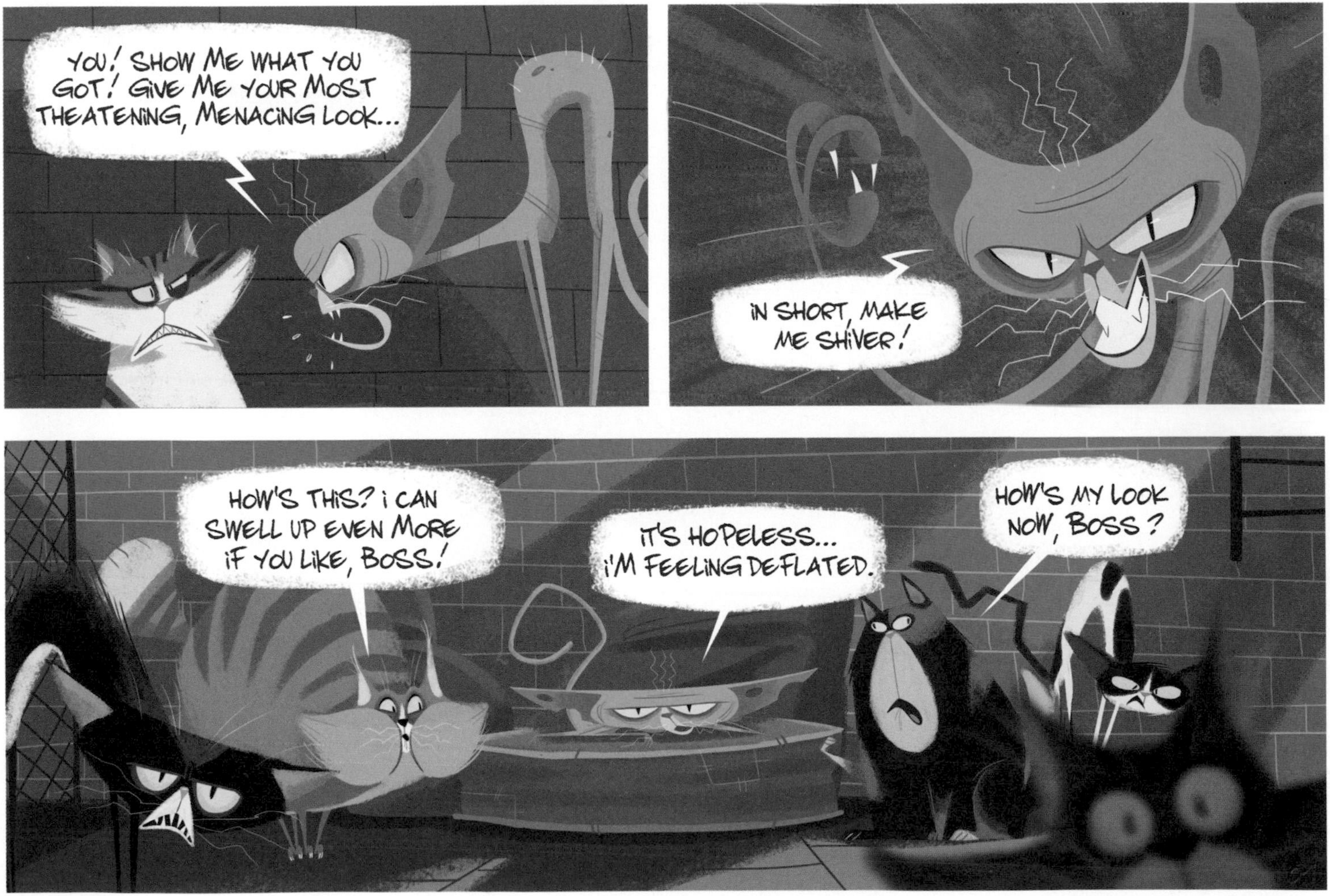
YOU! SHOW ME WHAT YOU GOT! GIVE ME YOUR MOST THEATENING, MENACING LOOK...
IN SHORT, MAKE ME SHIVER!
HOW'S THIS? I CAN SWELL UP EVEN MORE IF YOU LIKE, BOSS!
IT'S HOPELESS... I'M FEELING DEFLATED.
HOW'S MY LOOK NOW, BOSS?

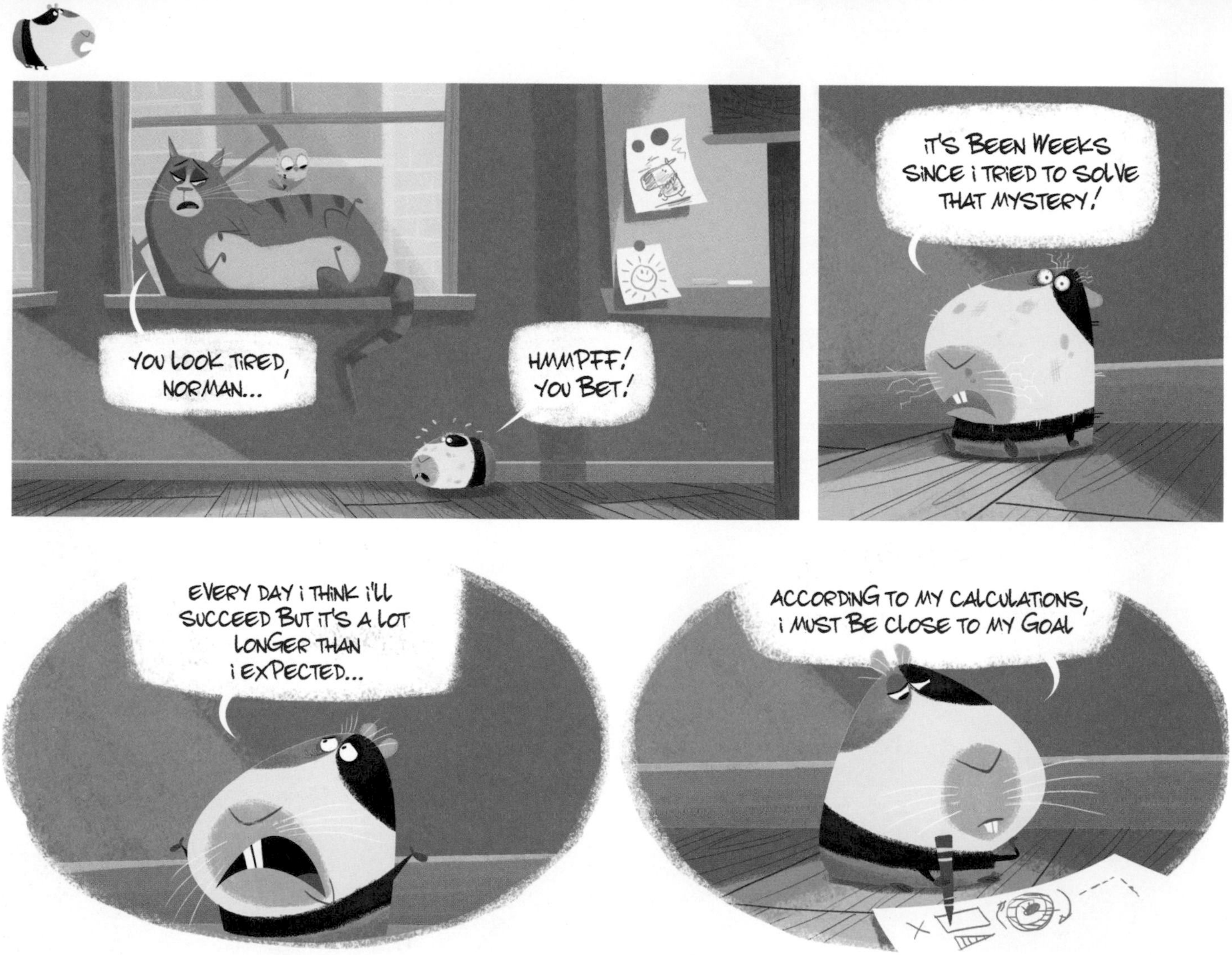
YOU LOOK TIRED, NORMAN...
HMMPFF! YOU BET!
IT'S BEEN WEEKS SINCE I TRIED TO SOLVE THAT MYSTERY!
EVERY DAY I THINK I'LL SUCCEED BUT IT'S A LOT LONGER THAN I EXPECTED...
ACCORDING TO MY CALCULATIONS, I MUST BE CLOSE TO MY GOAL

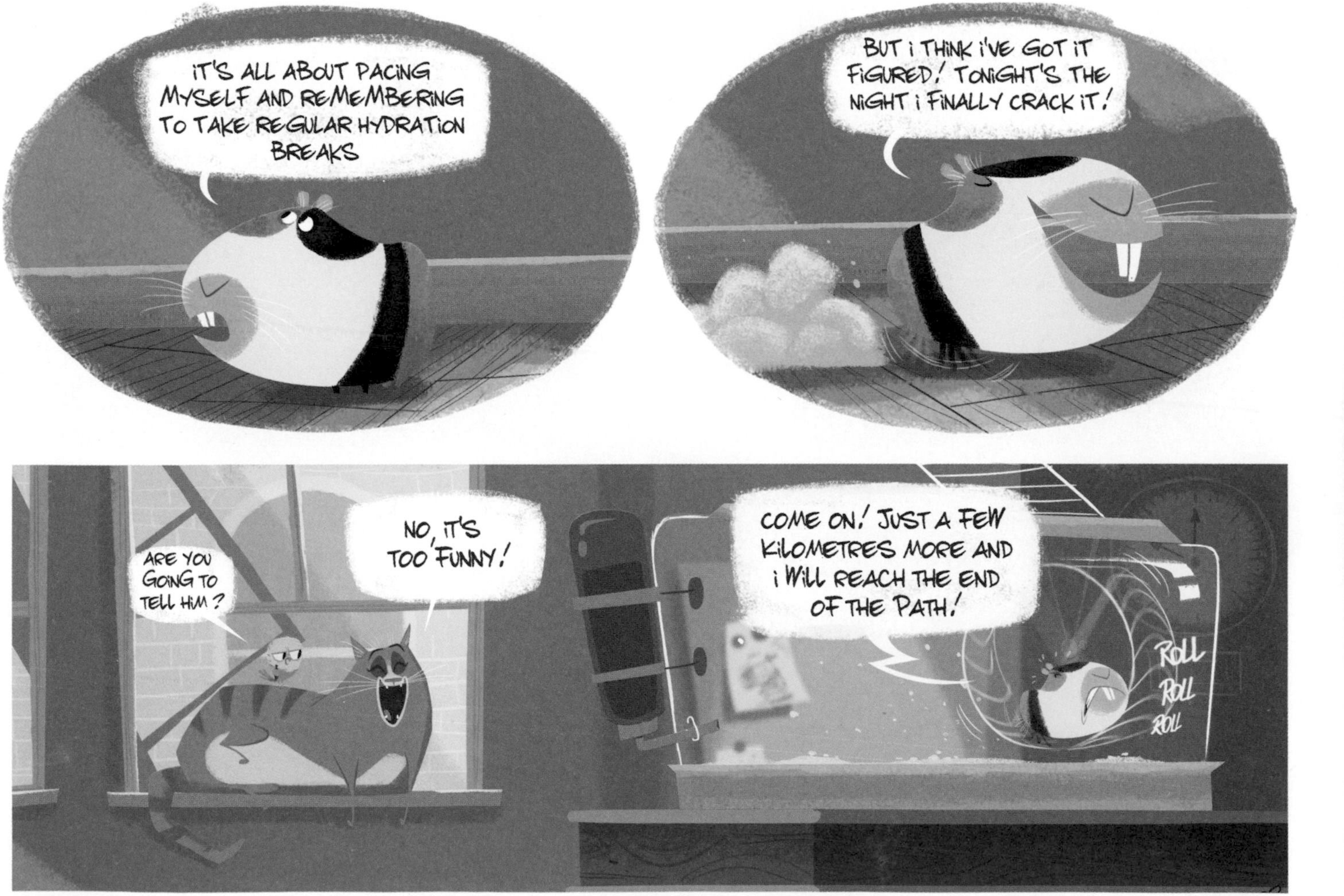
IT'S ALL ABOUT PACING MYSELF AND REMEMBERING TO TAKE REGULAR HYDRATION BREAKS
BUT I THINK I'VE GOT IT FIGURED! TONIGHT'S THE NIGHT I FINALLY CRACK IT!
ARE YOU GOING TO TELL HIM?
NO, IT'S TOO FUNNY!
COME ON! JUST A FEW KILOMETRES MORE AND I WILL REACH THE END OF THE PATH!
ROLL
ROLL
ROLL

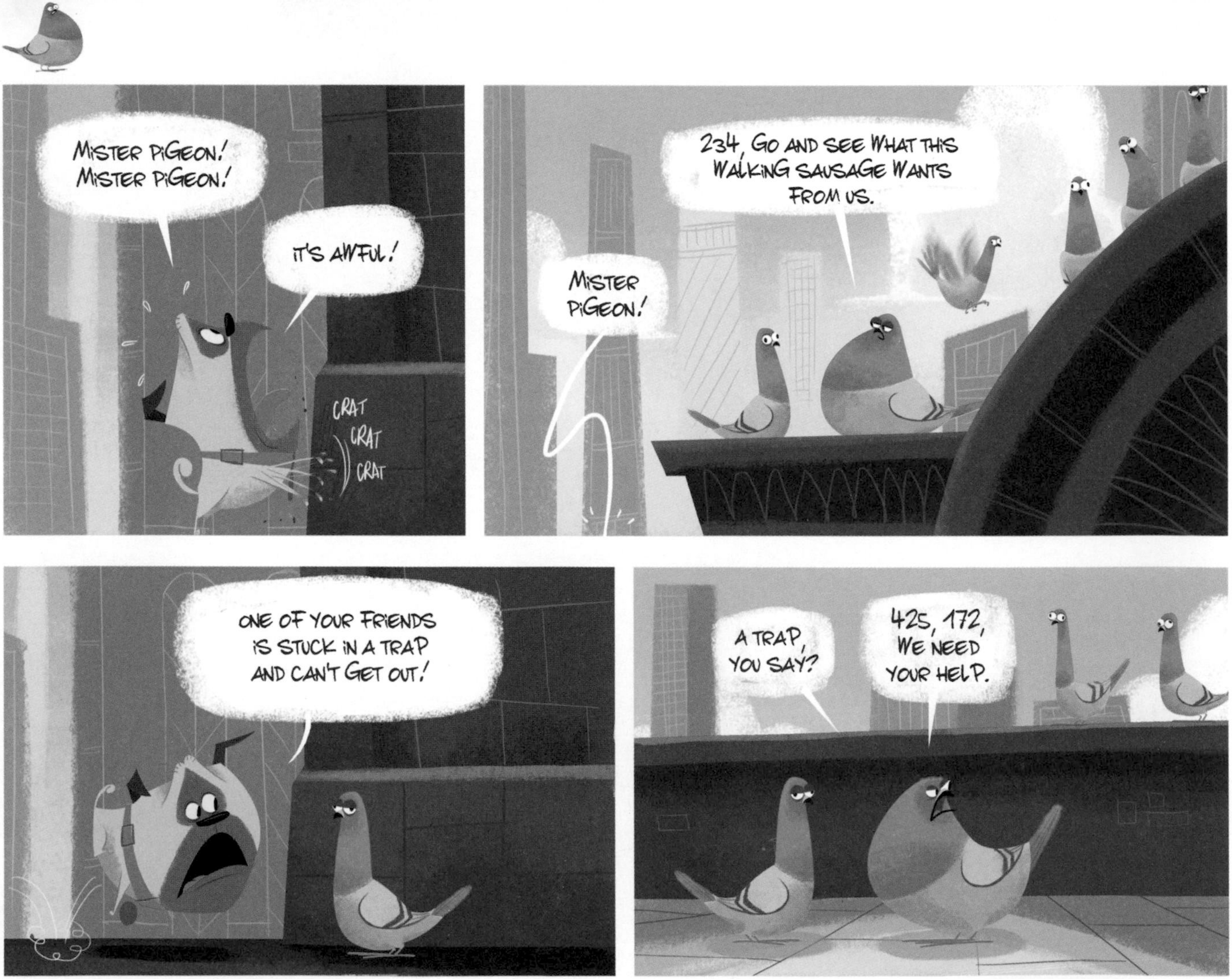
MISTER PIGEON! MISTER PIGEON!
IT'S AWFUL!
CRAT CRAT CRAT
MISTER PIGEON!
234, GO AND SEE WHAT THIS WALKING SAUSAGE WANTS FROM US.
ONE OF YOUR FRIENDS IS STUCK IN A TRAP AND CAN'T GET OUT!
A TRAP, YOU SAY?
425, 172, WE NEED YOUR HELP.

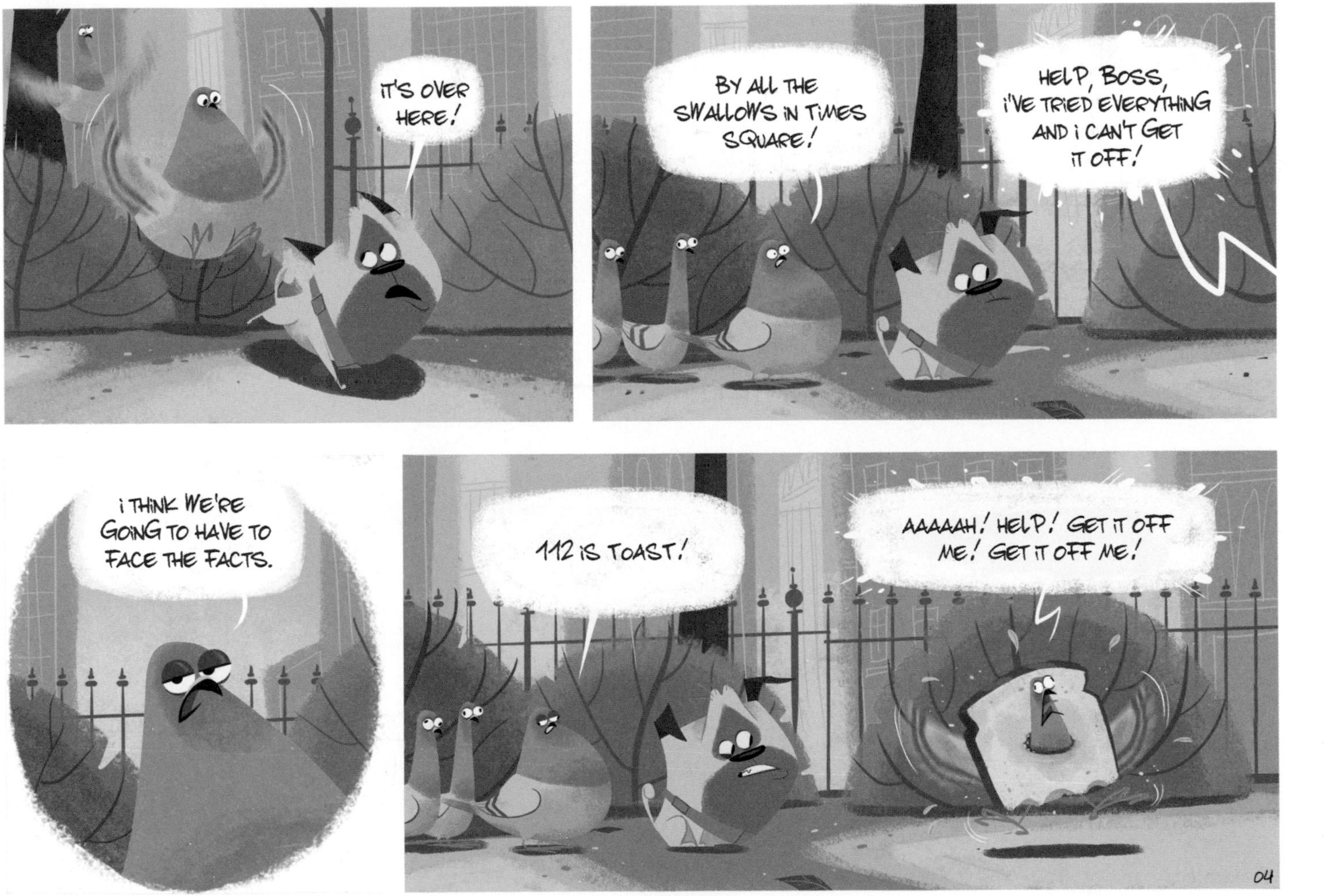
IT'S OVER HERE!
BY ALL THE SWALLOWS IN TIMES SQUARE!
HELP, BOSS, I'VE TRIED EVERYTHING AND I CAN'T GET IT OFF!
I THINK WE'RE GOING TO HAVE TO FACE THE FACTS.
112 IS TOAST!
AAAAAH! HELP! GET IT OFF ME! GET IT OFF ME!

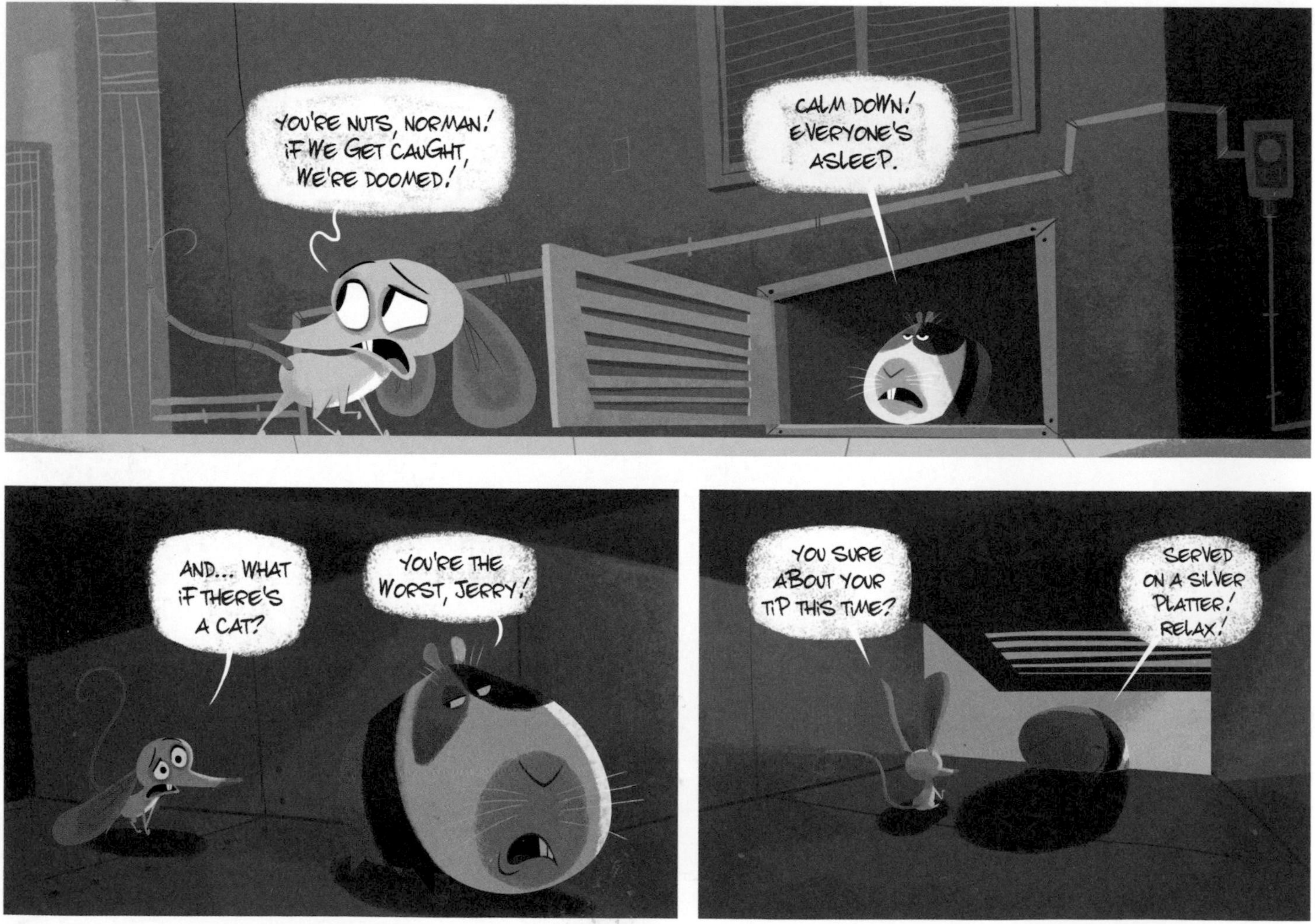
YOU'RE NUTS, NORMAN! IF WE GET CAUGHT, WE'RE DOOMED!
CALM DOWN! EVERYONE'S ASLEEP.
AND... WHAT IF THERE'S A CAT?
YOU'RE THE WORST, JERRY!
YOU SURE ABOUT YOUR TIP THIS TIME?
SERVED ON A SILVER PLATTER! RELAX!

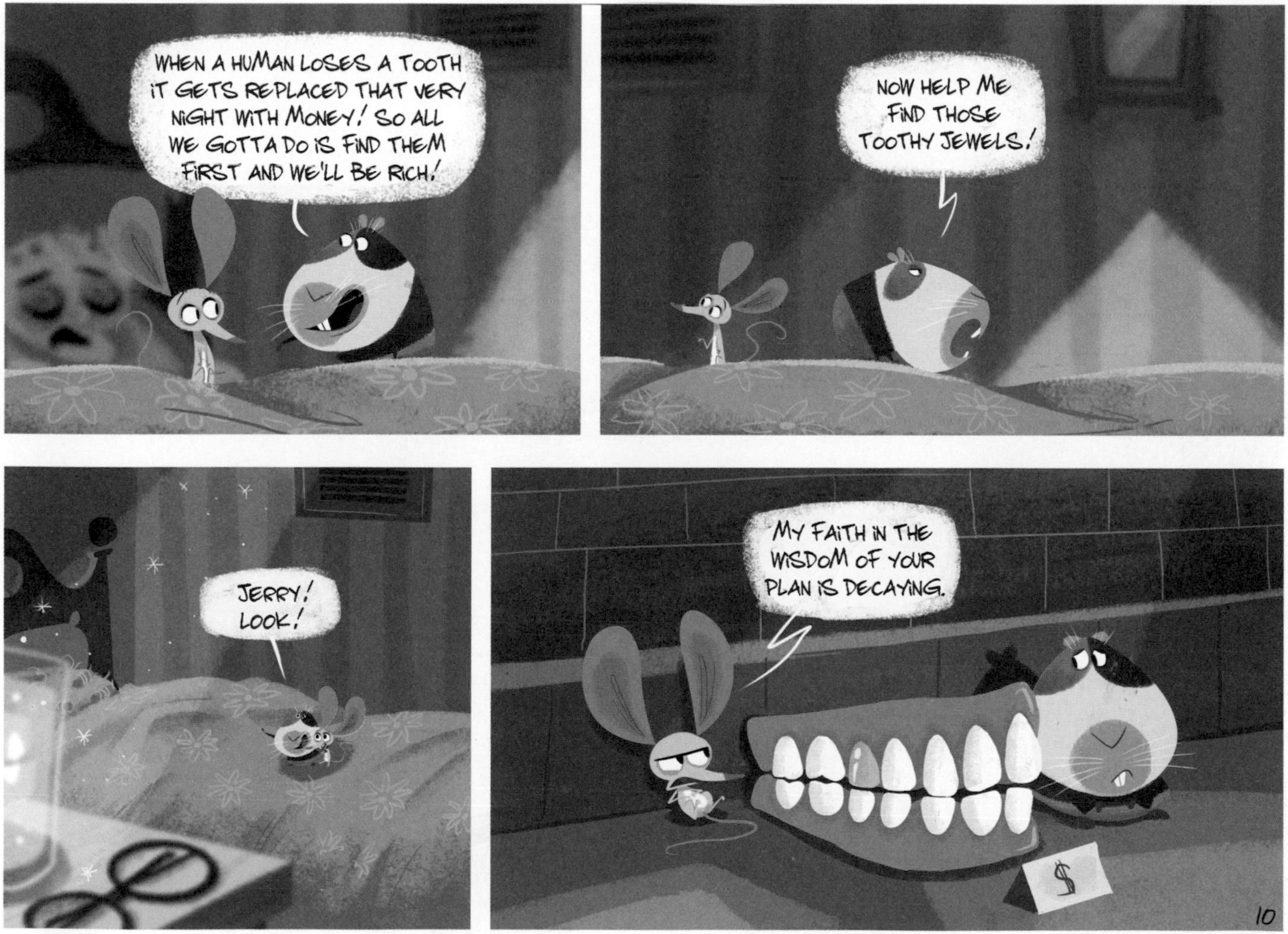
WHEN A HUMAN LOSES A TOOTH IT GETS REPLACED THAT VERY NIGHT WITH MONEY! SO ALL WE GOTTA DO IS FIND THEM FIRST AND WE'LL BE RICH!
NOW HELP ME FIND THOSE TOOTHY JEWELS!
JERRY! LOOK!
MY FAITH IN THE WISDOM OF YOUR PLAN IS DECAYING.
$

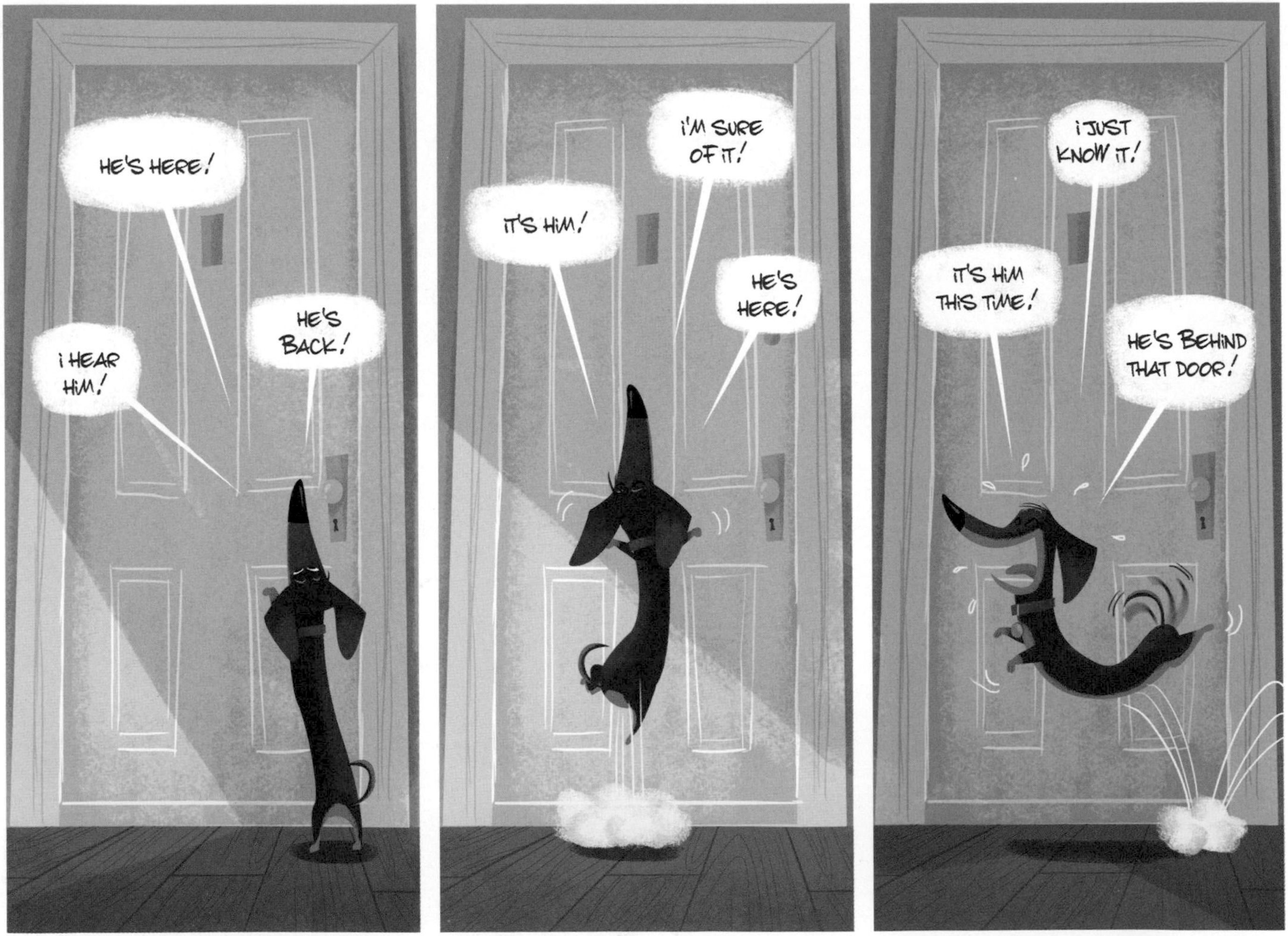
HE'S HERE!
HE'S BACK!
I HEAR HIM!
I'M SURE OF IT!
IT'S HIM!
HE'S HERE!
I JUST KNOW IT!
IT'S HIM THIS TIME!
HE'S BEHIND THAT DOOR!

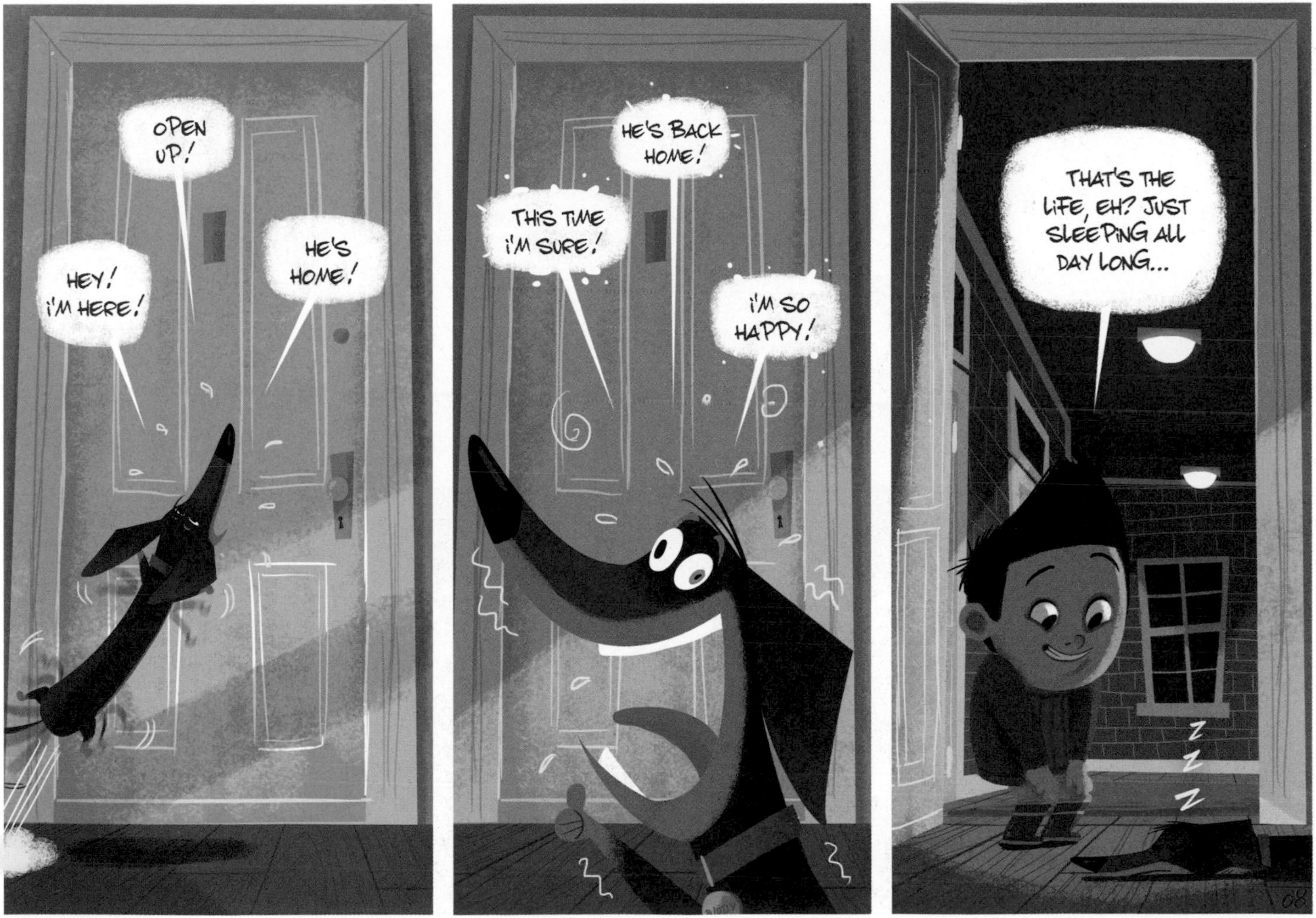
OPEN UP!
HEY! I'M HERE!
HE'S HOME!
HE'S BACK HOME!
THIS TIME I'M SURE!
I'M SO HAPPY!
THAT'S THE LIFE, EH? JUST SLEEPING ALL DAY LONG...
Z Z Z

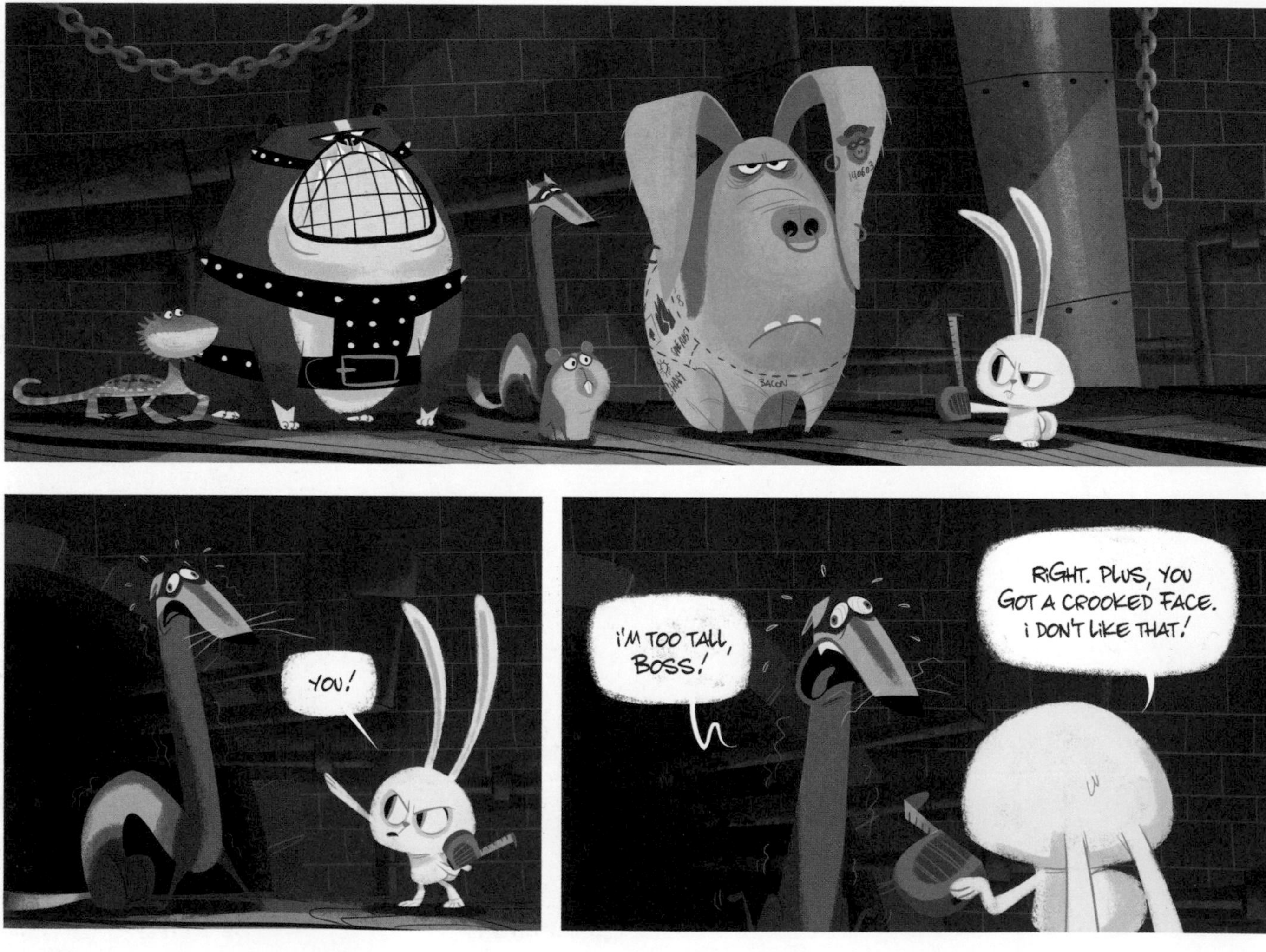
YOU!
I'M TOO TALL, BOSS!
RIGHT. PLUS, YOU GOT A CROOKED FACE. I DON'T LIKE THAT!

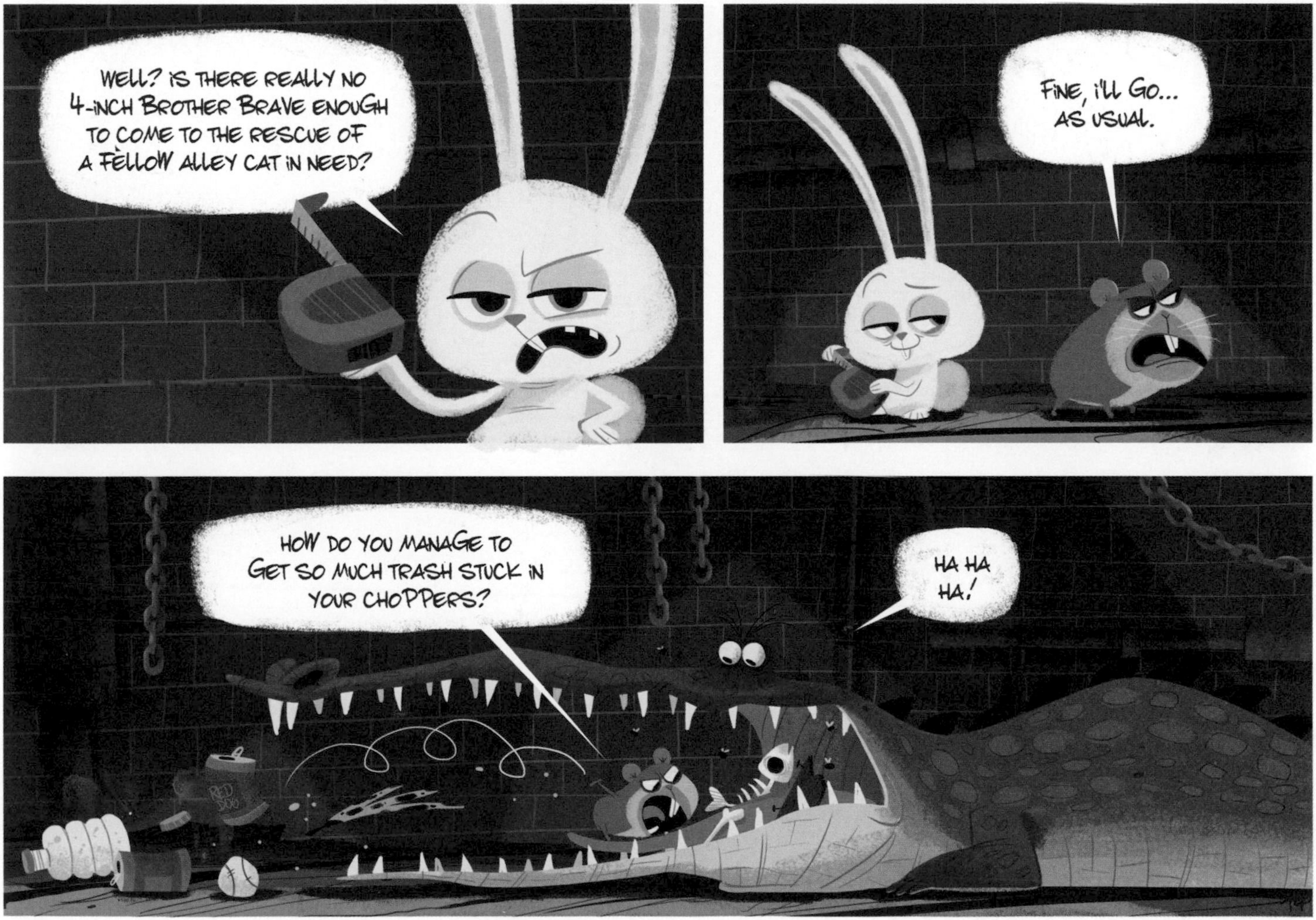
WELL? IS THERE REALLY NO 4-INCH BROTHER BRAVE ENOUGH TO COME TO THE RESCUE OF A FELLOW ALLEY CAT IN NEED?
FINE, I'LL GO... AS USUAL.
HOW DO YOU MANAGE TO GET SO MUCH TRASH STUCK IN YOUR CHOPPERS?
HA HA HA!

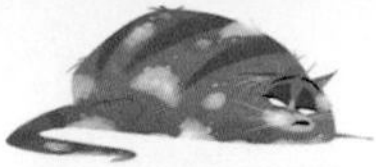

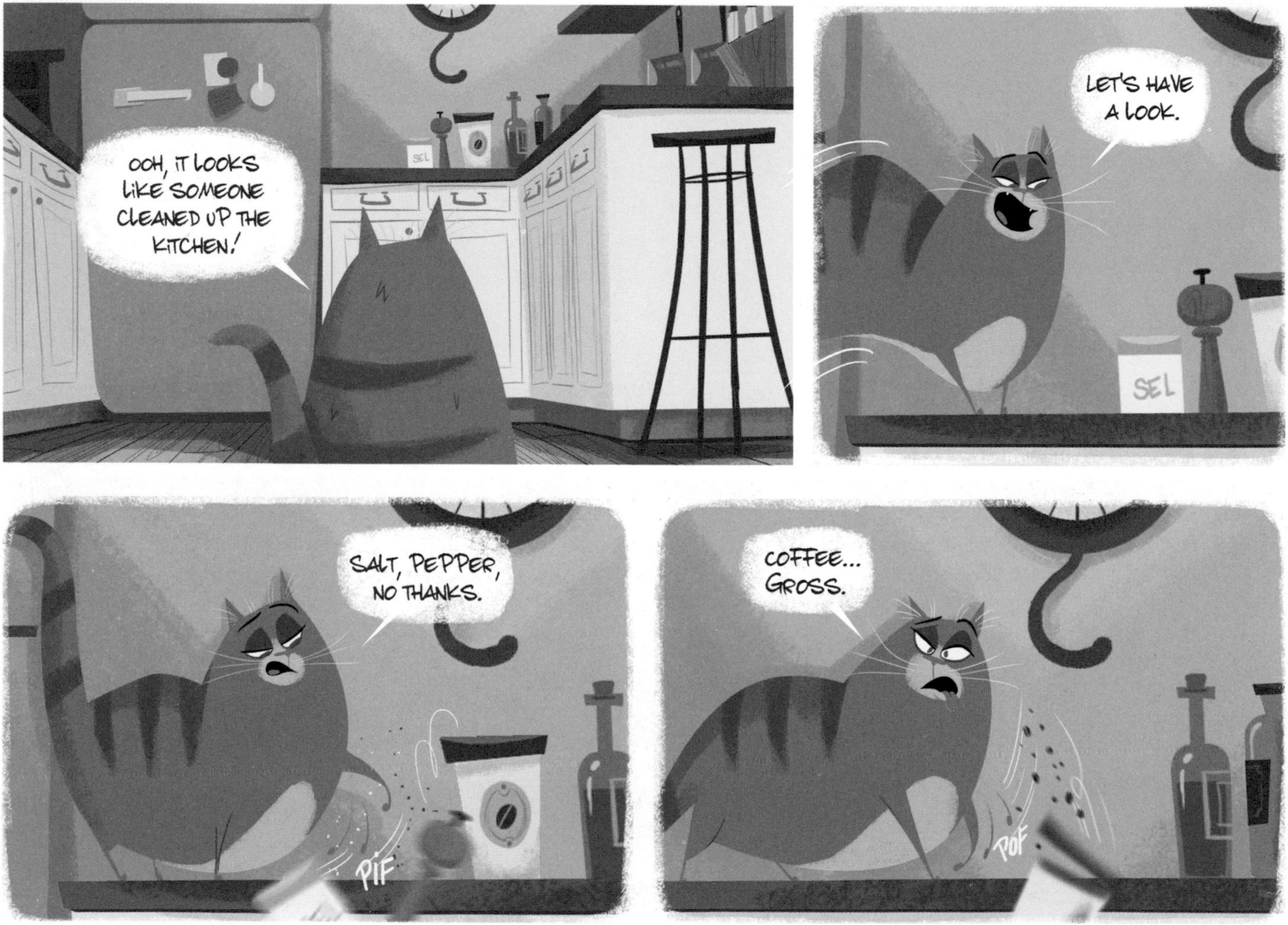
SEL
OOH, IT LOOKS LIKE SOMEONE CLEANED UP THE KITCHEN!
LET'S HAVE A LOOK.
SEL
SALT, PEPPER, NO THANKS.
PIF
COFFEE... GROSS.
POF

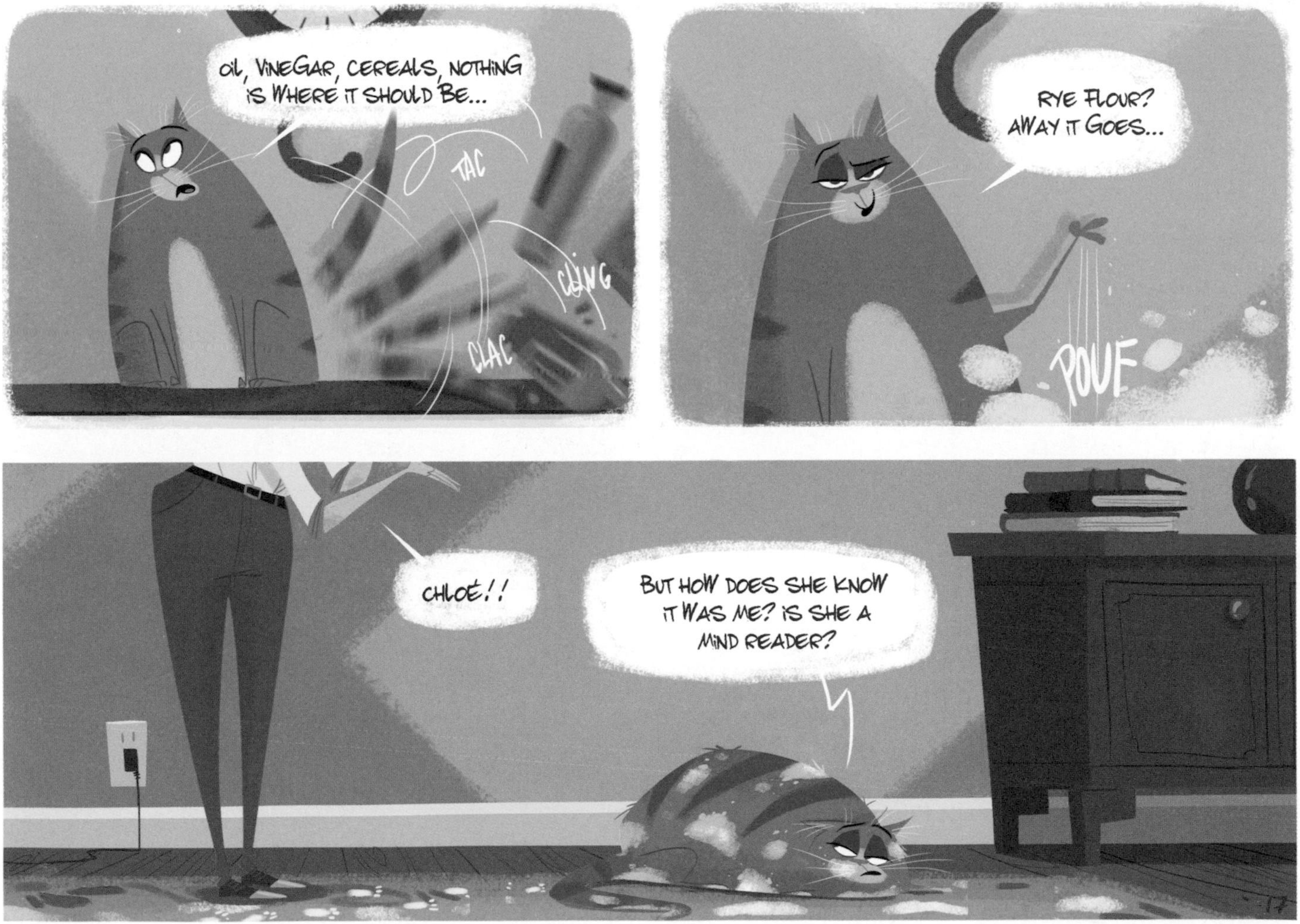
OIL, VINEGAR, CEREALS, NOTHING IS WHERE IT SHOULD BE...
TAC
CLING
CLAC
RYE FLOUR? AWAY IT GOES...
POUF
CHLOÉ!!
BUT HOW DOES SHE KNOW IT WAS ME? IS SHE A MIND READER?

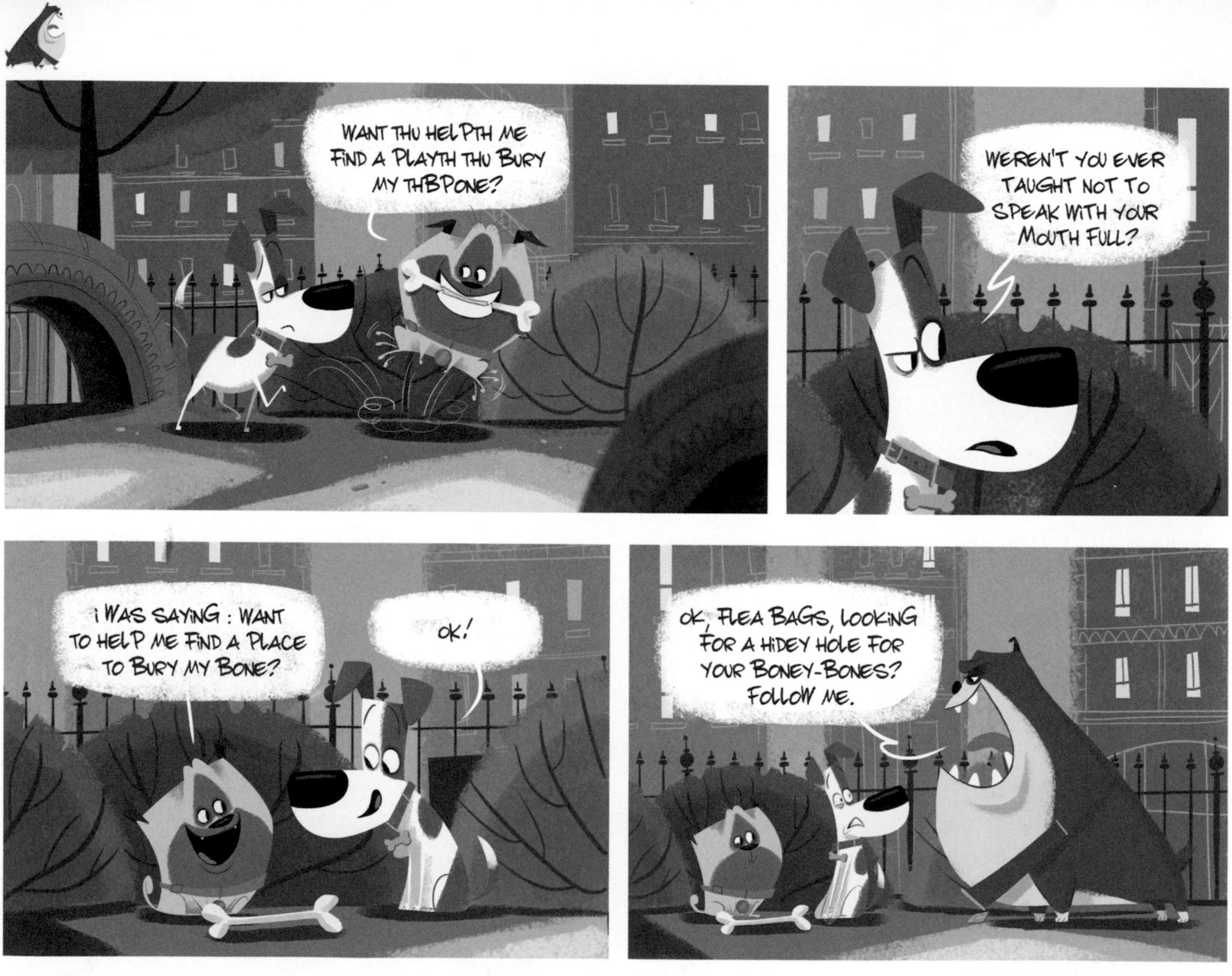
WANT THU HELPTH ME FIND A PLAYTH THU BURY MY THBPONE?
WEREN'T YOU EVER TAUGHT NOT TO SPEAK WITH YOUR MOUTH FULL?
I WAS SAYING : WANT TO HELP ME FIND A PLACE TO BURY MY BONE?
OK!
OK, FLEA BAGS, LOOKING FOR A HIDEY HOLE FOR YOUR BONEY-BONES? FOLLOW ME.

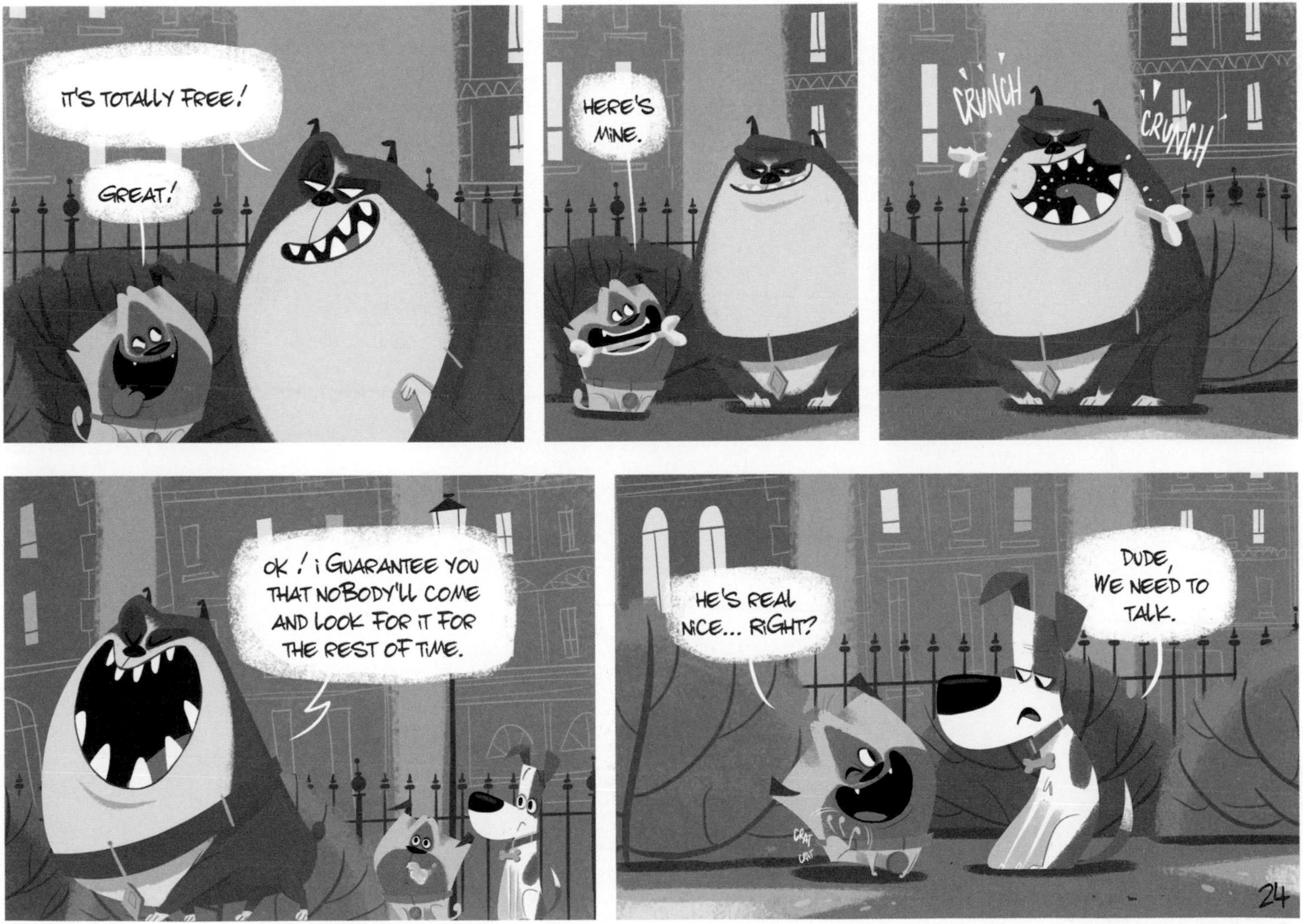
IT'S TOTALLY FREE!
GREAT!
HERE'S MINE.
CRUNCH
CRUNCH
OK! I GUARANTEE YOU THAT NOBODY'LL COME AND LOOK FOR IT FOR THE REST OF TIME.
HE'S REAL NICE... RIGHT?
DUDE, WE NEED TO TALK.

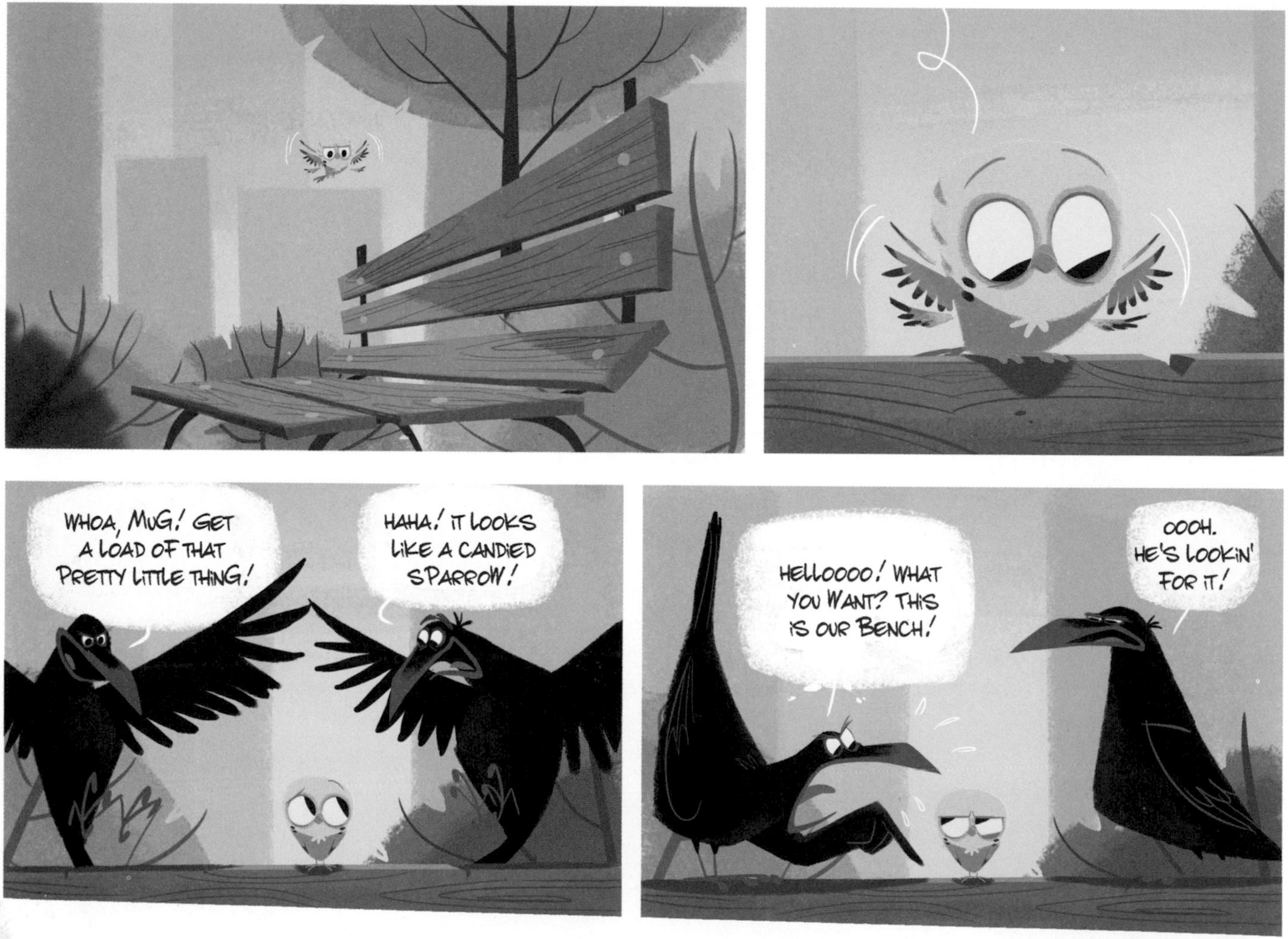
WHOA, MUG! GET A LOAD OF THAT PRETTY LITTLE THING!
HAHA! IT LOOKS LIKE A CANDIED SPARROW!
HELLOOOO! WHAT YOU WANT? THIS IS OUR BENCH!
OOOH. HE'S LOOKIN' FOR IT!

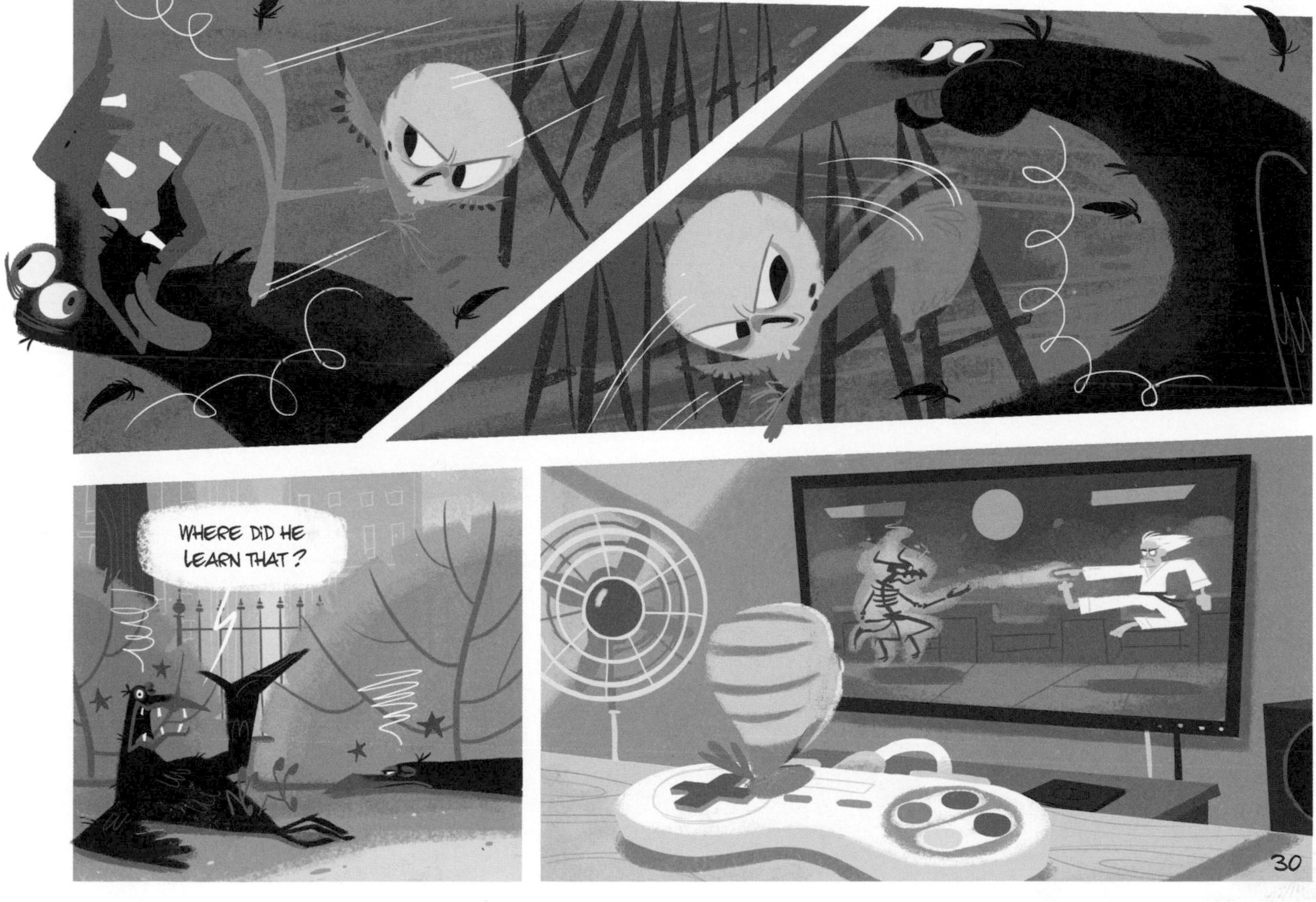
KYAAAAH
WHERE DID HE LEARN THAT?

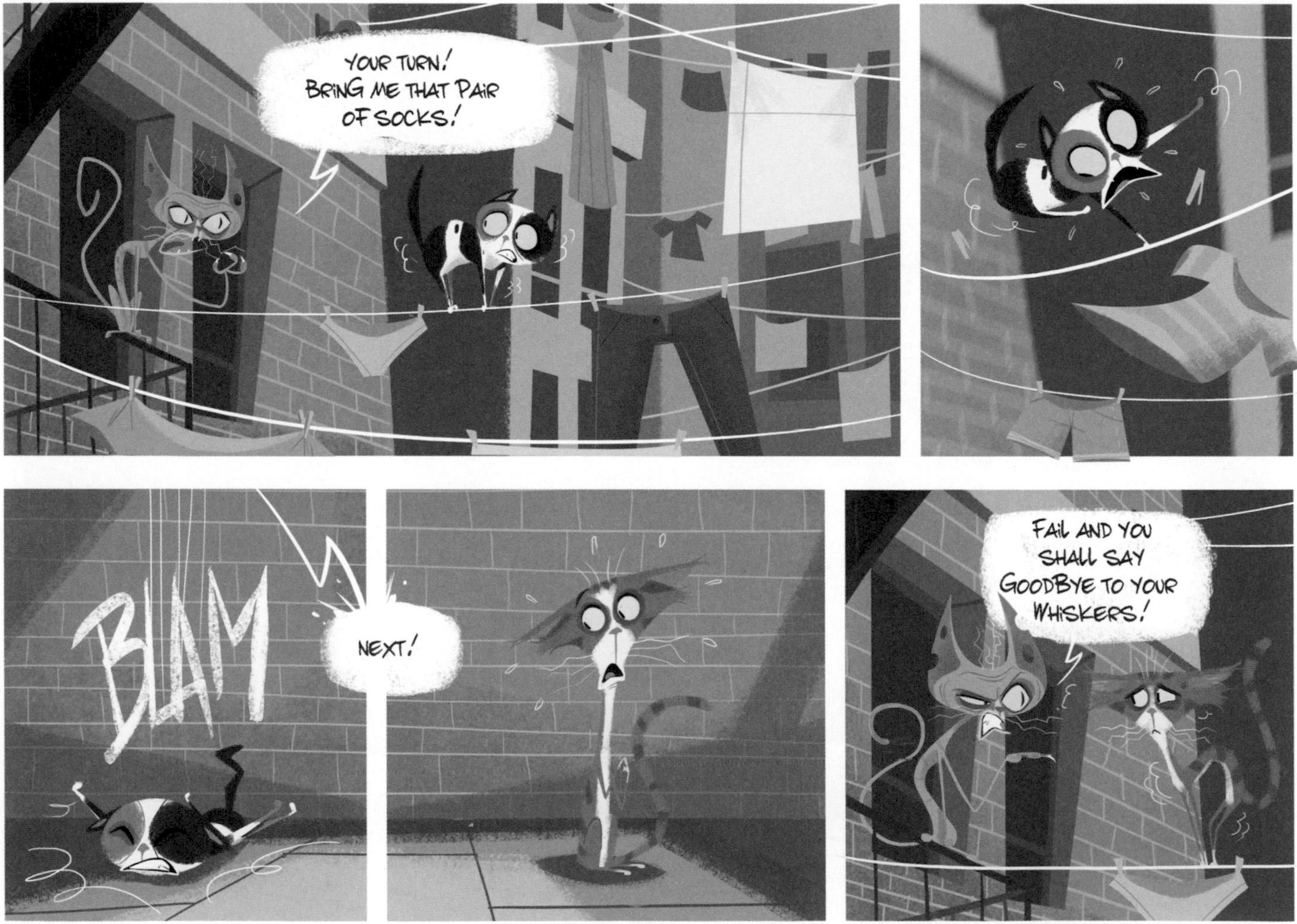
YOUR TURN! BRING ME THAT PAIR OF SOCKS!
BLAM
NEXT!
FAIL AND YOU SHALL SAY GOODBYE TO YOUR WHISKERS!

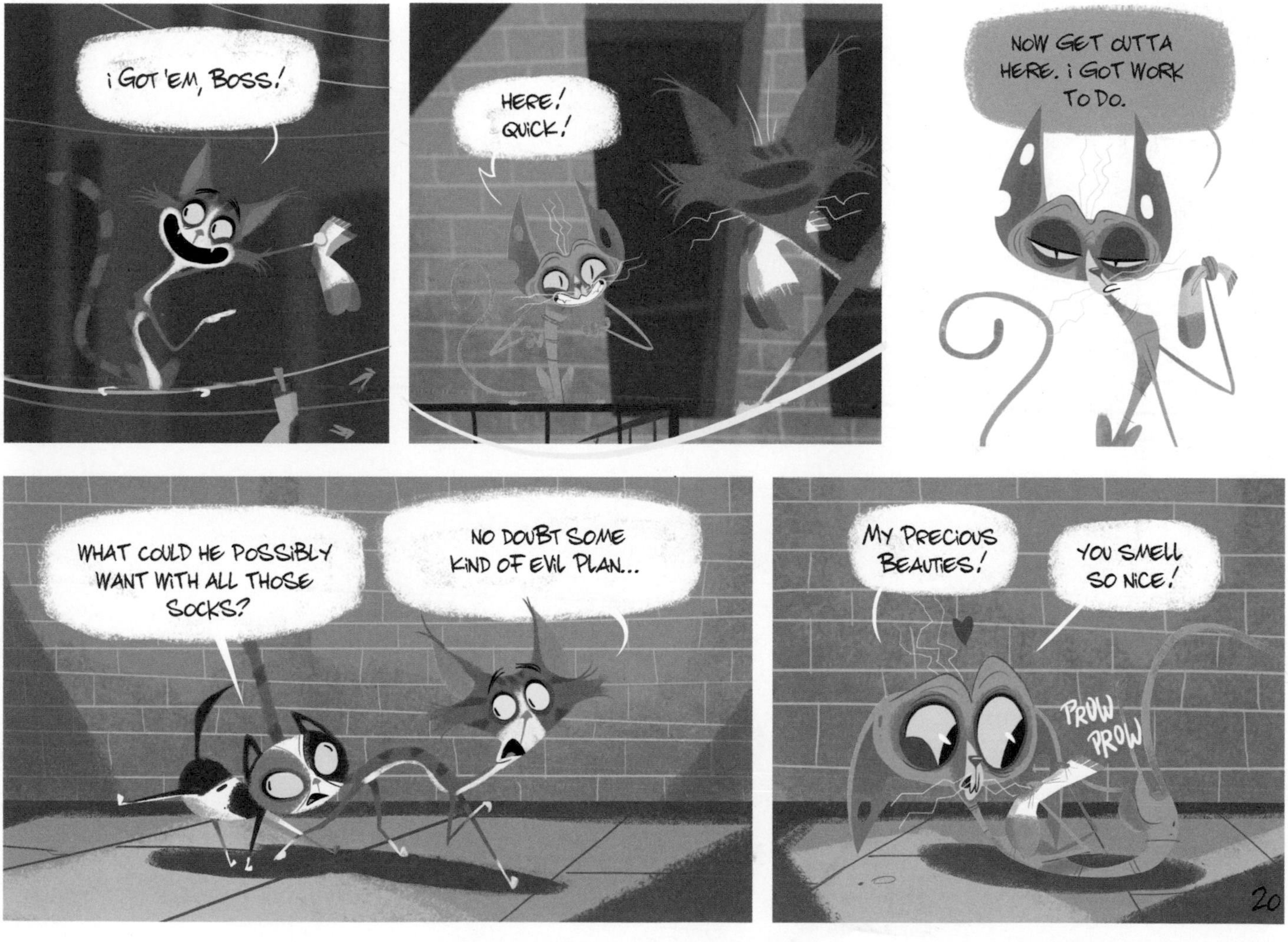
I GOT 'EM, BOSS!
HERE! QUICK!
NOW GET OUTTA HERE. I GOT WORK TO DO.
WHAT COULD HE POSSIBLY WANT WITH ALL THOSE SOCKS?
NO DOUBT SOME KIND OF EVIL PLAN...
MY PRECIOUS BEAUTIES!
YOU SMELL SO NICE!
PROW
PROW

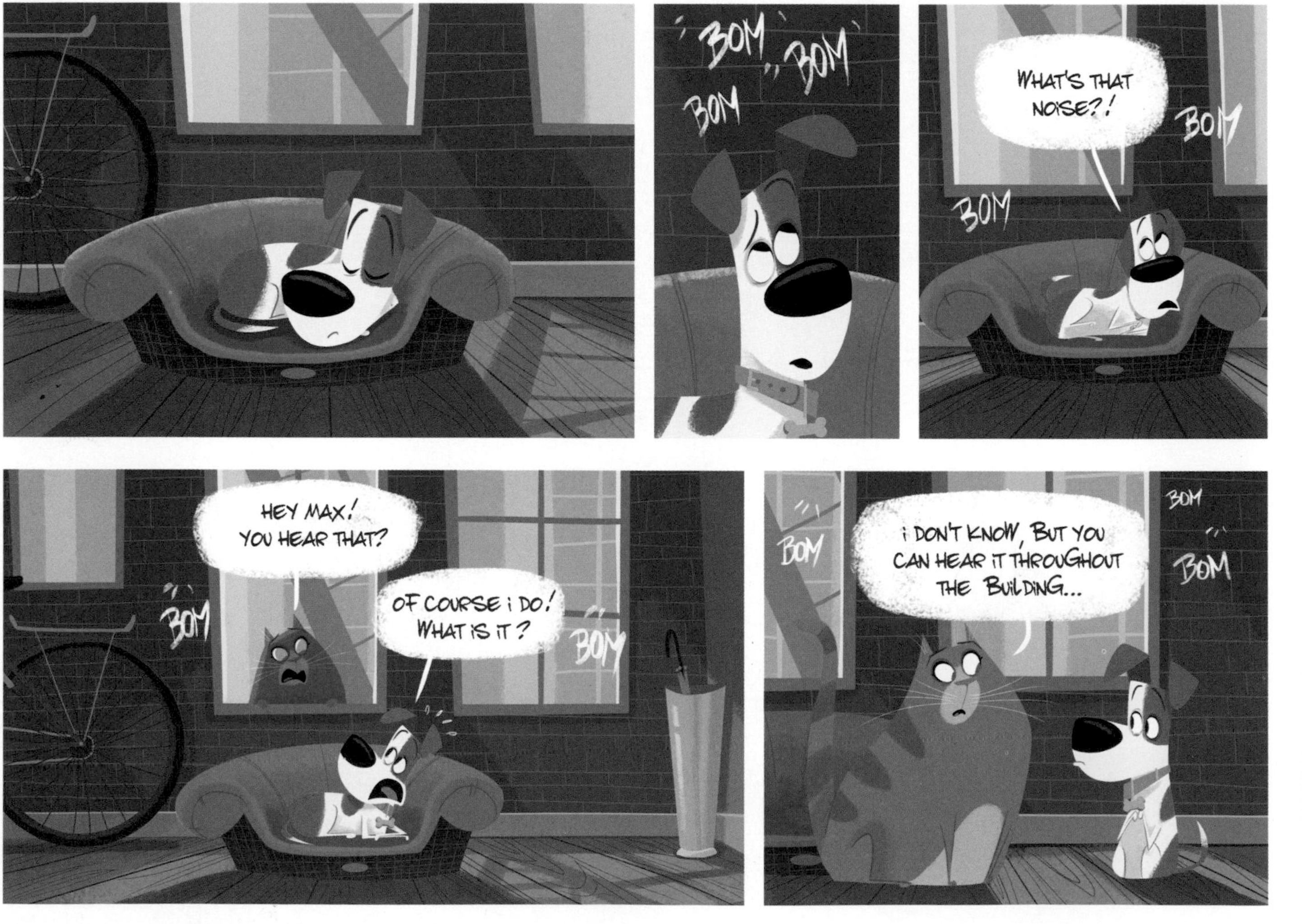
BOM
BOM
BOM
WHAT'S THAT NOISE?!
BOM
BOM
HEY MAX! YOU HEAR THAT?
BOM
OF COURSE I DO! WHAT IS IT?
BOM
BOM
I DON'T KNOW, BUT YOU CAN HEAR IT THROUGHOUT THE BUILDING...
BOM
BOM

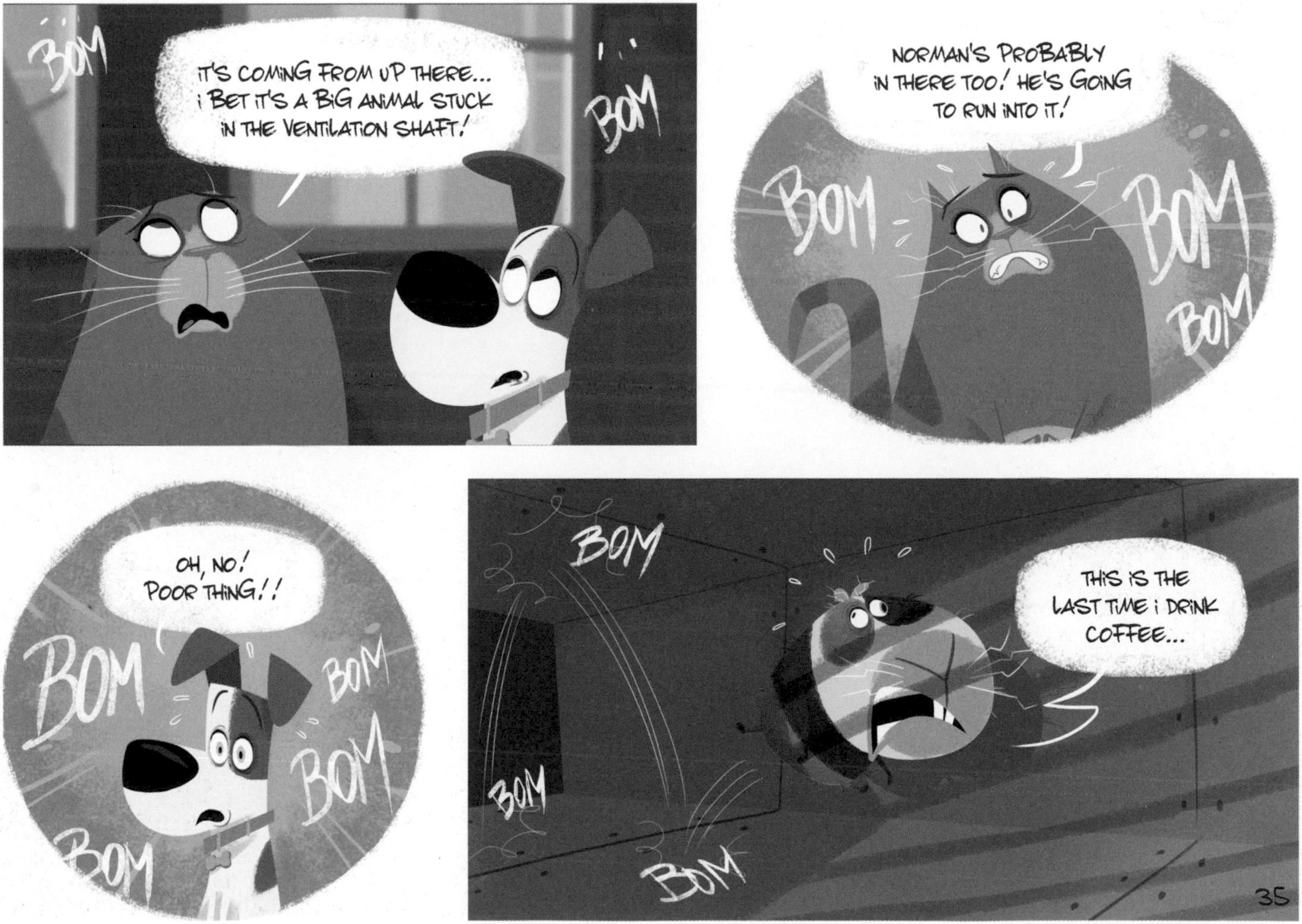
BOM
IT'S COMING FROM UP THERE... I BET IT'S A BIG ANIMAL STUCK IN THE VENTILATION SHAFT!
BOM
NORMAN'S PROBABLY IN THERE TOO! HE'S GOING TO RUN INTO IT!
BOM
BOM
BOM
OH, NO! POOR THING!!
BOM
BOM
BOM
BOM
BOM
THIS IS THE LAST TIME I DRINK COFFEE...
BOM
BOM

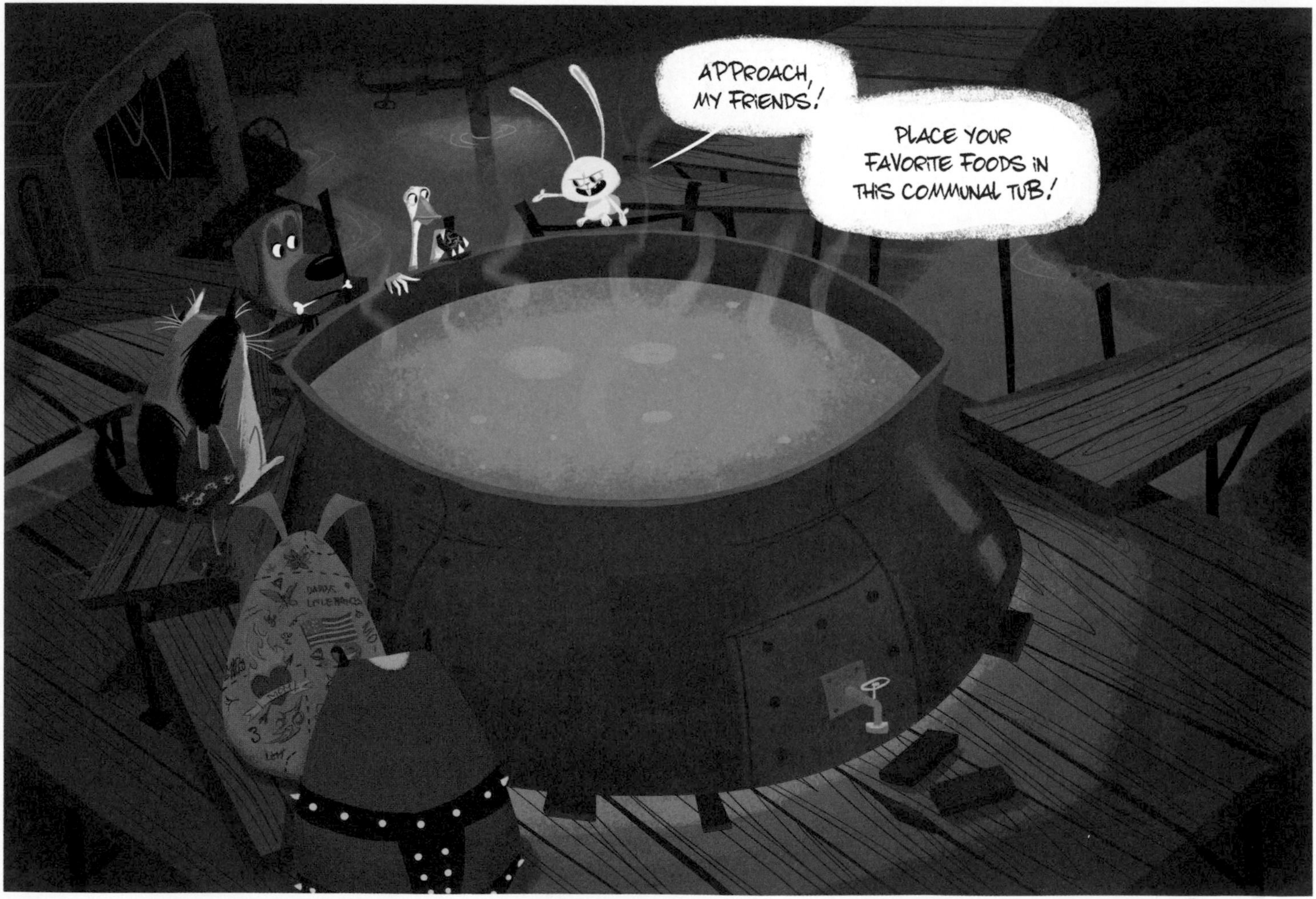
APPROACH, MY FRIENDS!
PLACE YOUR FAVORITE FOODS IN THIS COMMUNAL TUB!

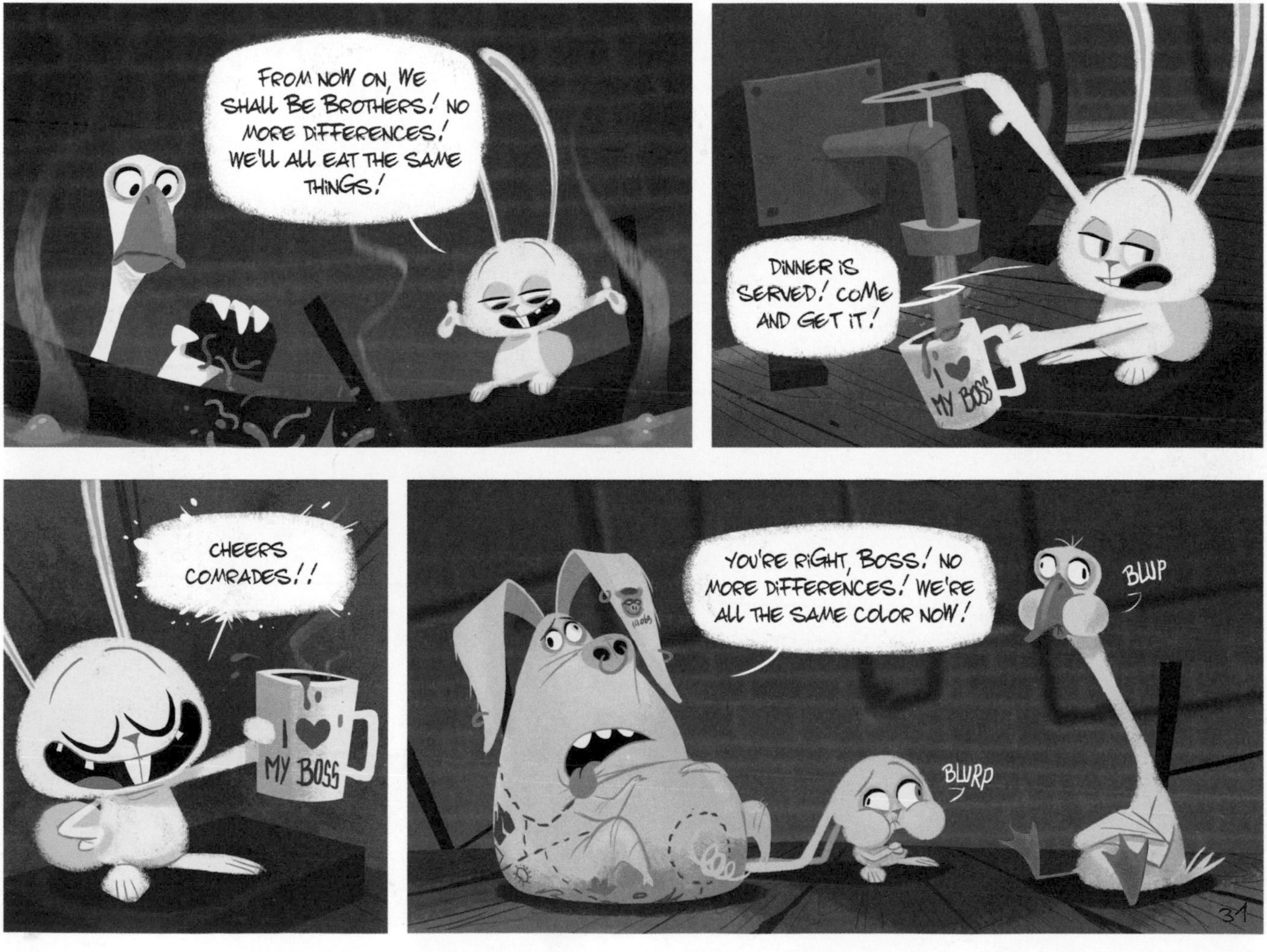

FROM NOW ON, WE SHALL BE BROTHERS! NO MORE DIFFERENCES! WE'LL ALL EAT THE SAME THINGS!
DINNER IS SERVED! COME AND GET IT!
I ♥ MY BOSS
CHEERS COMRADES!!
I ♥ MY BOSS
YOU'RE RIGHT, BOSS! NO MORE DIFFERENCES! WE'RE ALL THE SAME COLOR NOW!
BLUP
BLURP

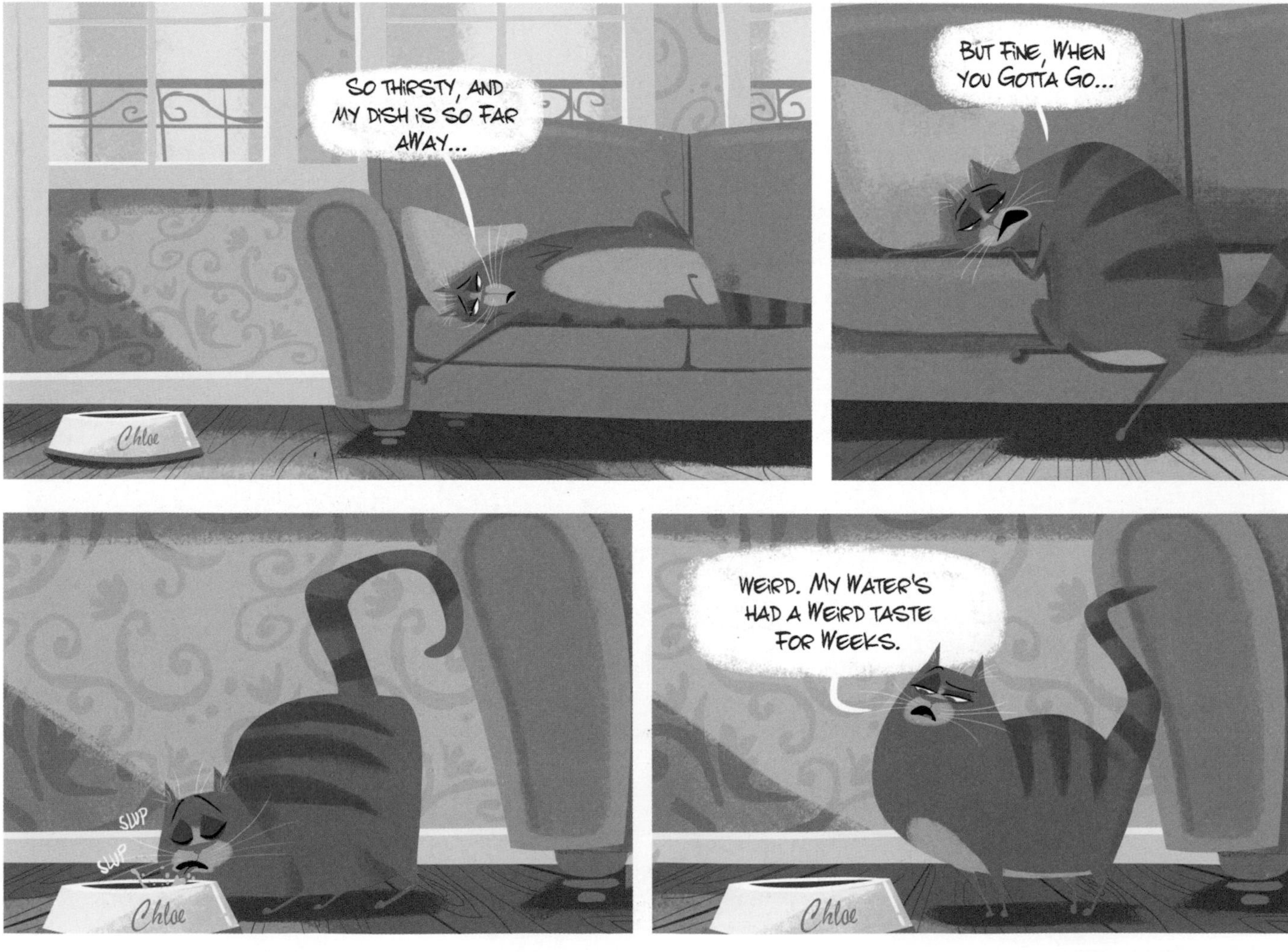
SO THIRSTY, AND MY DISH IS SO FAR AWAY...
Chloe
BUT FINE, WHEN YOU GOTTA GO...
SLUP
SLUP
Chloe
WEIRD. MY WATER'S HAD A WEIRD TASTE FOR WEEKS.
Chloe

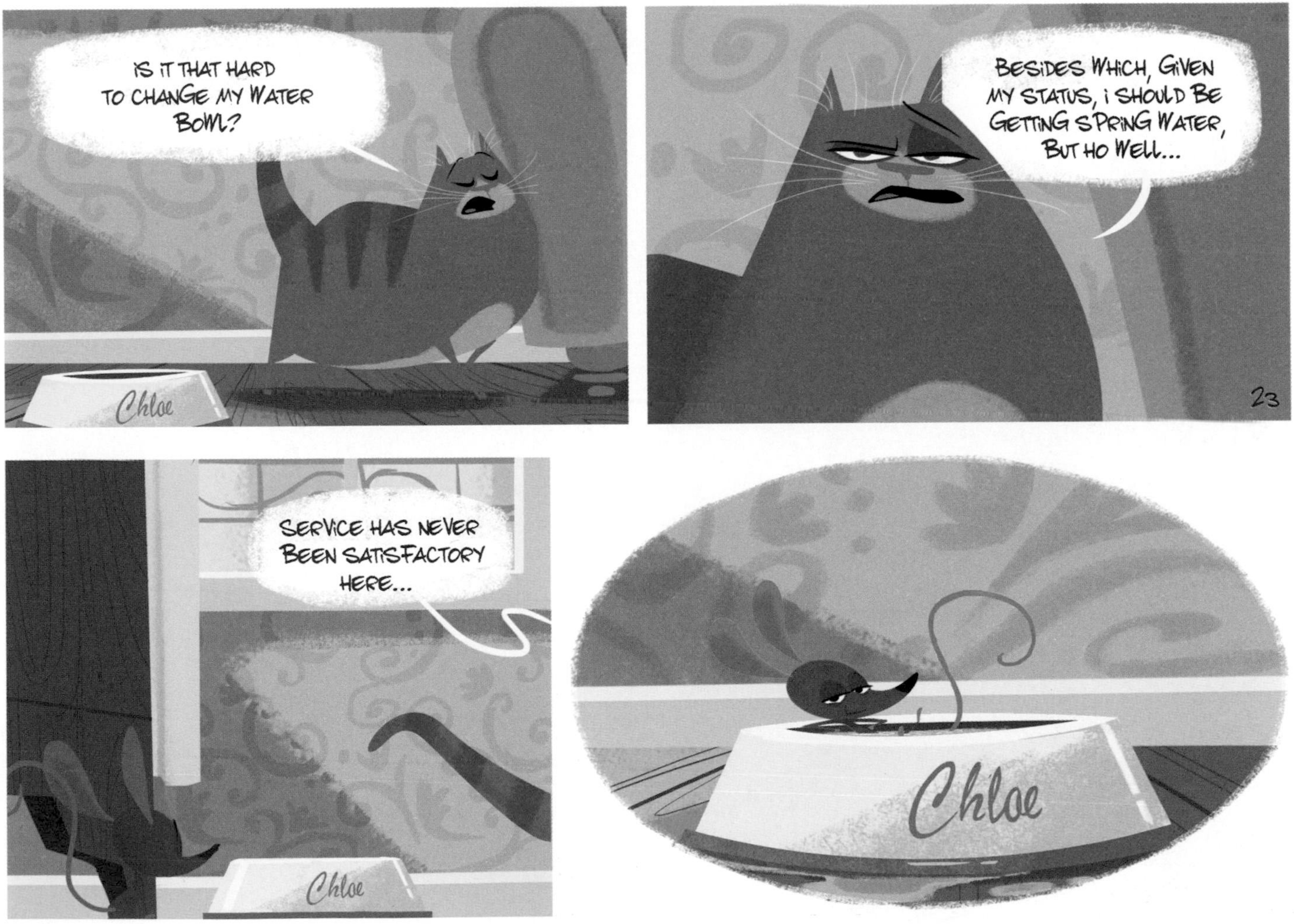
IS IT THAT HARD TO CHANGE MY WATER BOWL?
Chloe
BESIDES WHICH, GIVEN MY STATUS, I SHOULD BE GETTING SPRING WATER, BUT HO WELL...
SERVICE HAS NEVER BEEN SATISFACTORY HERE...
Chloe
Chloe

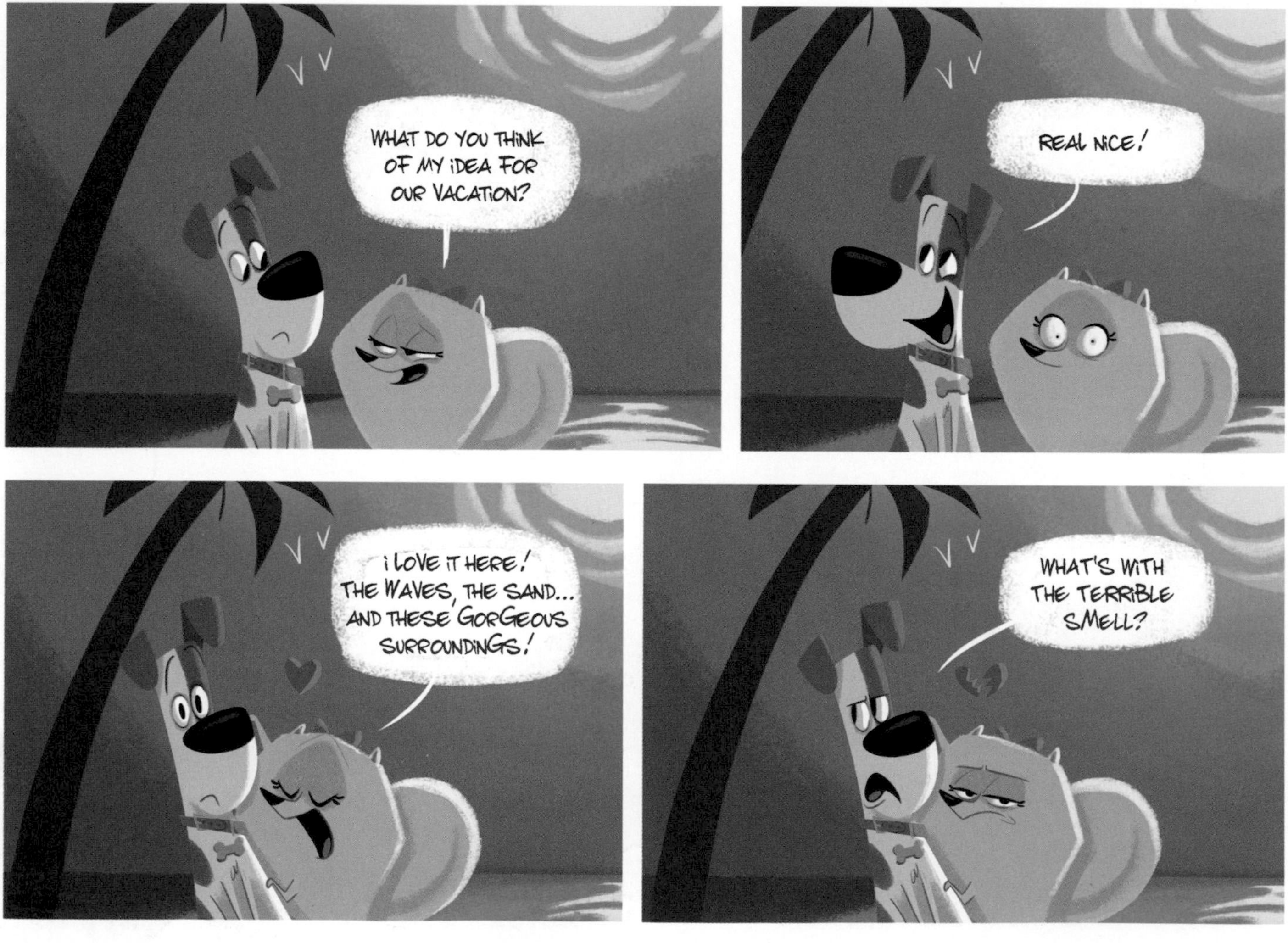
WHAT DO YOU THINK OF MY IDEA FOR OUR VACATION?
REAL NICE!
I LOVE IT HERE! THE WAVES, THE SAND... AND THESE GORGEOUS SURROUNDINGS!
WHAT'S WITH THE TERRIBLE SMELL?

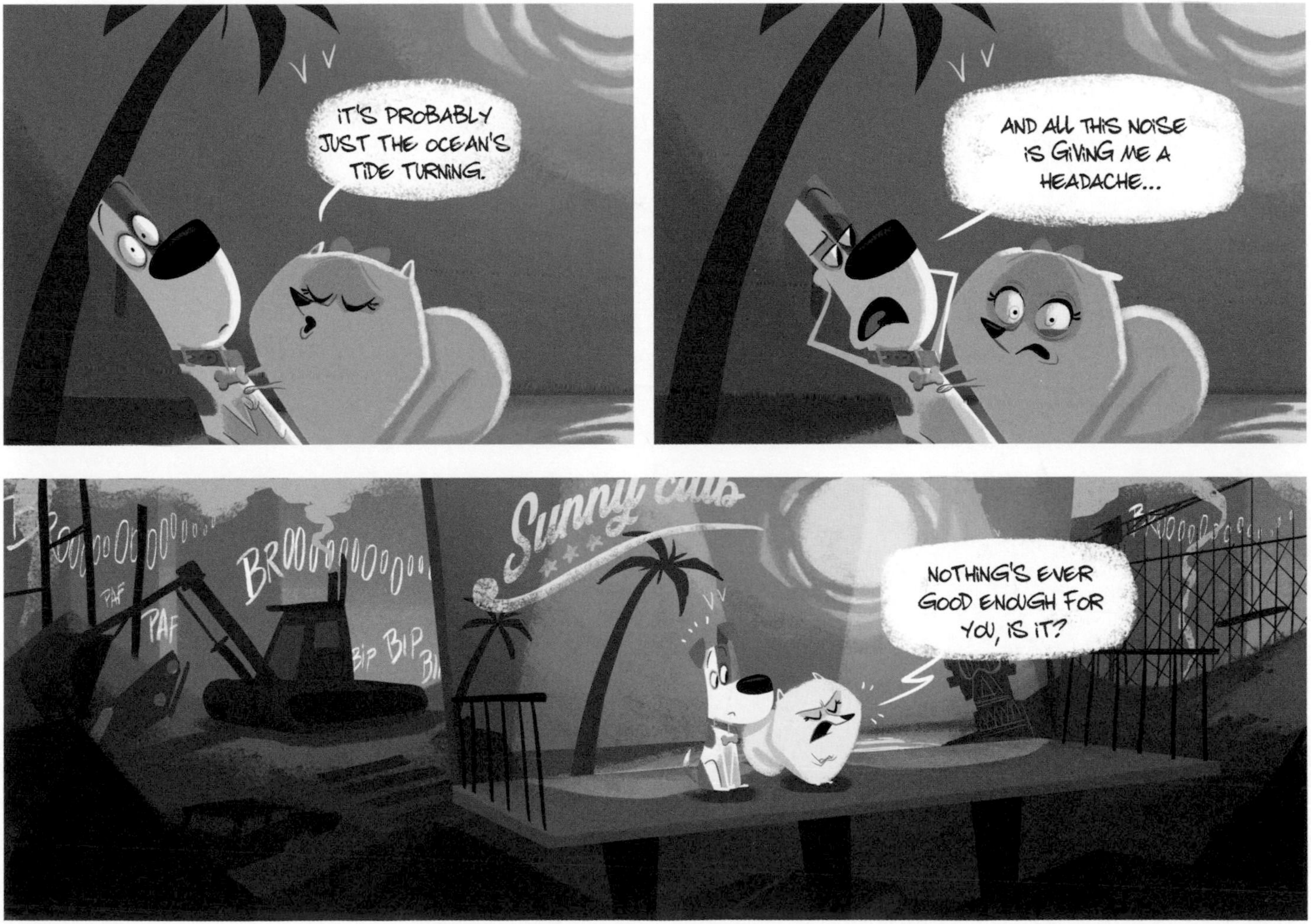
IT'S PROBABLY JUST THE OCEAN'S TIDE TURNING.
AND ALL THIS NOISE IS GIVING ME A HEADACHE...
PAF
PAF
BIP BIP
NOTHING'S EVER GOOD ENOUGH FOR YOU, IS IT?

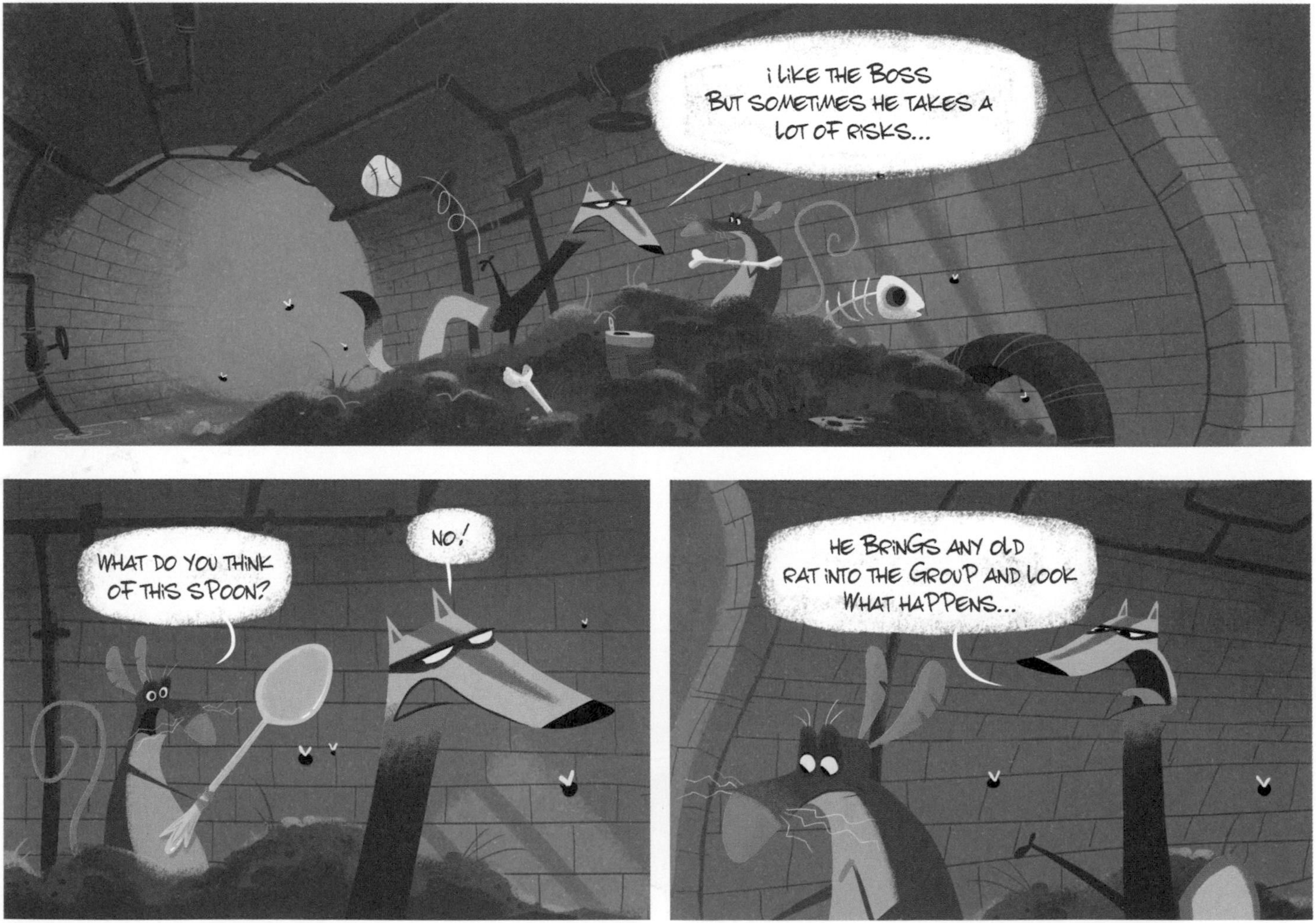
I LIKE THE BOSS BUT SOMETIMES HE TAKES A LOT OF RISKS...
WHAT DO YOU THINK OF THIS SPOON?
NO!
HE BRINGS ANY OLD RAT INTO THE GROUP AND LOOK WHAT HAPPENS...

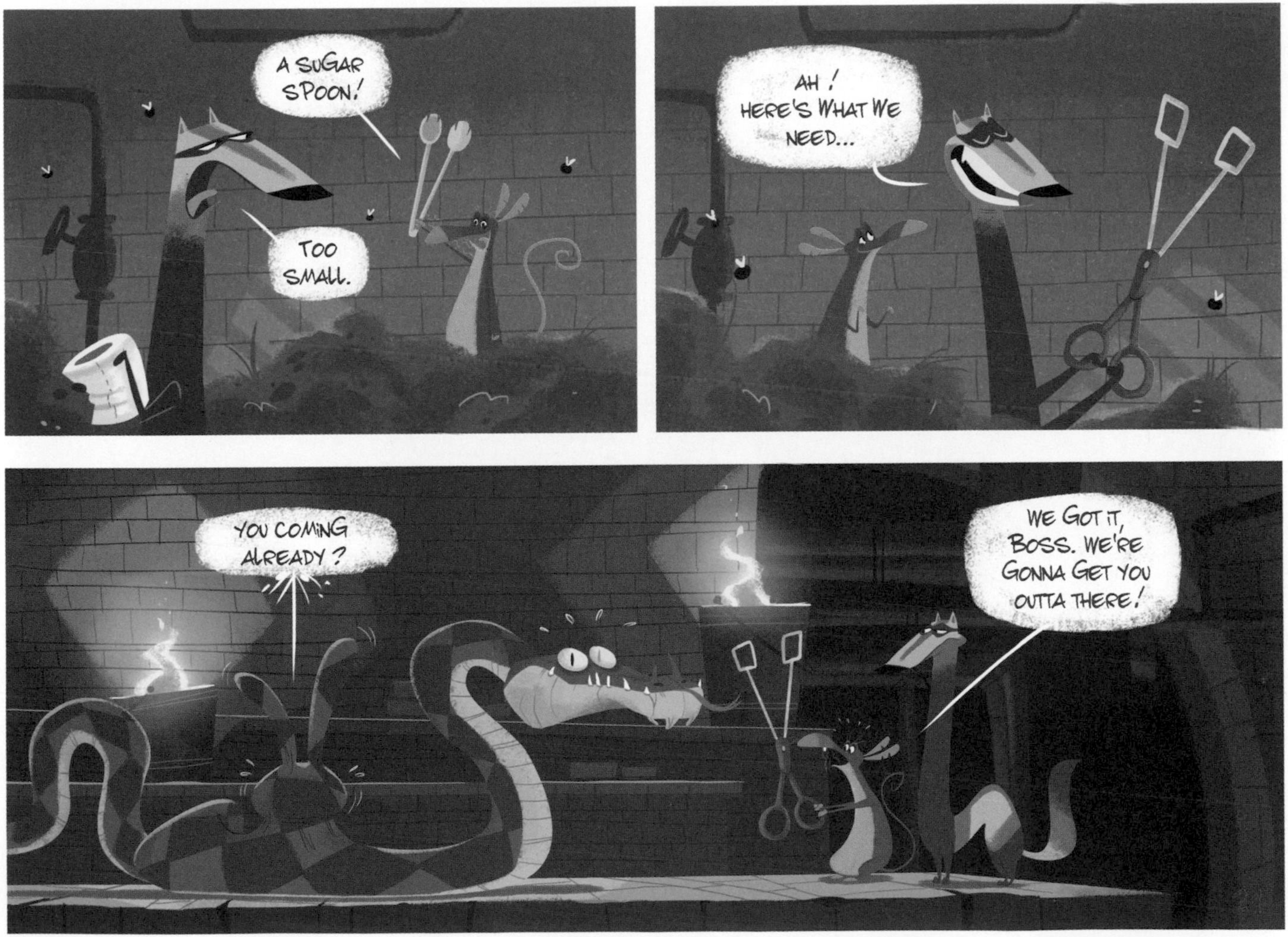
A SUGAR SPOON!
TOO SMALL.
AH! HERE'S WHAT WE NEED...
YOU COMING ALREADY?
WE GOT IT, BOSS. WE'RE GONNA GET YOU OUTTA THERE!

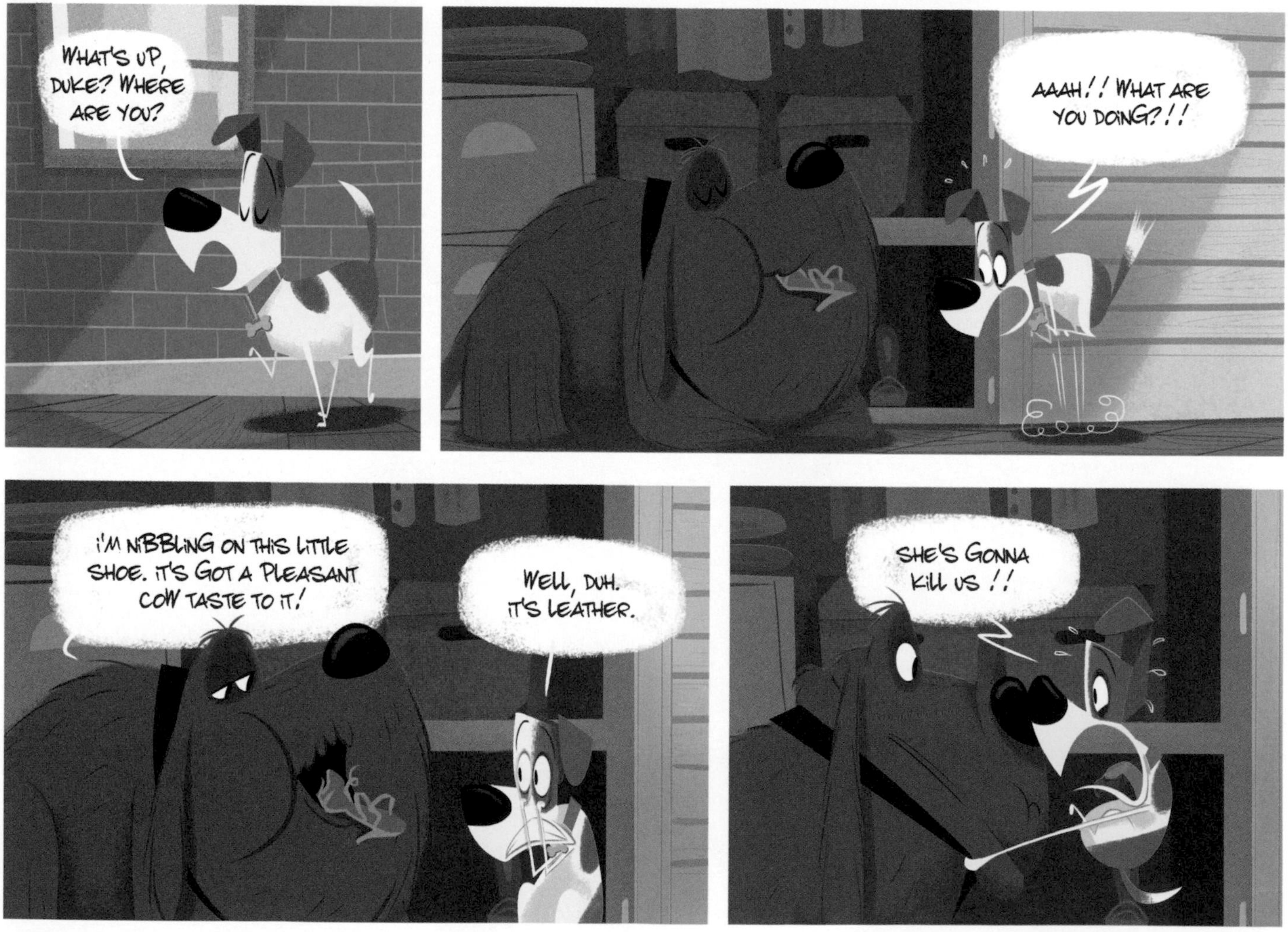
WHAT'S UP, DUKE? WHERE ARE YOU?
AAAH!! WHAT ARE YOU DOING?!!
I'M NIBBLING ON THIS LITTLE SHOE. IT'S GOT A PLEASANT COW TASTE TO IT!
WELL, DUH. IT'S LEATHER.
SHE'S GONNA KILL US!!

34

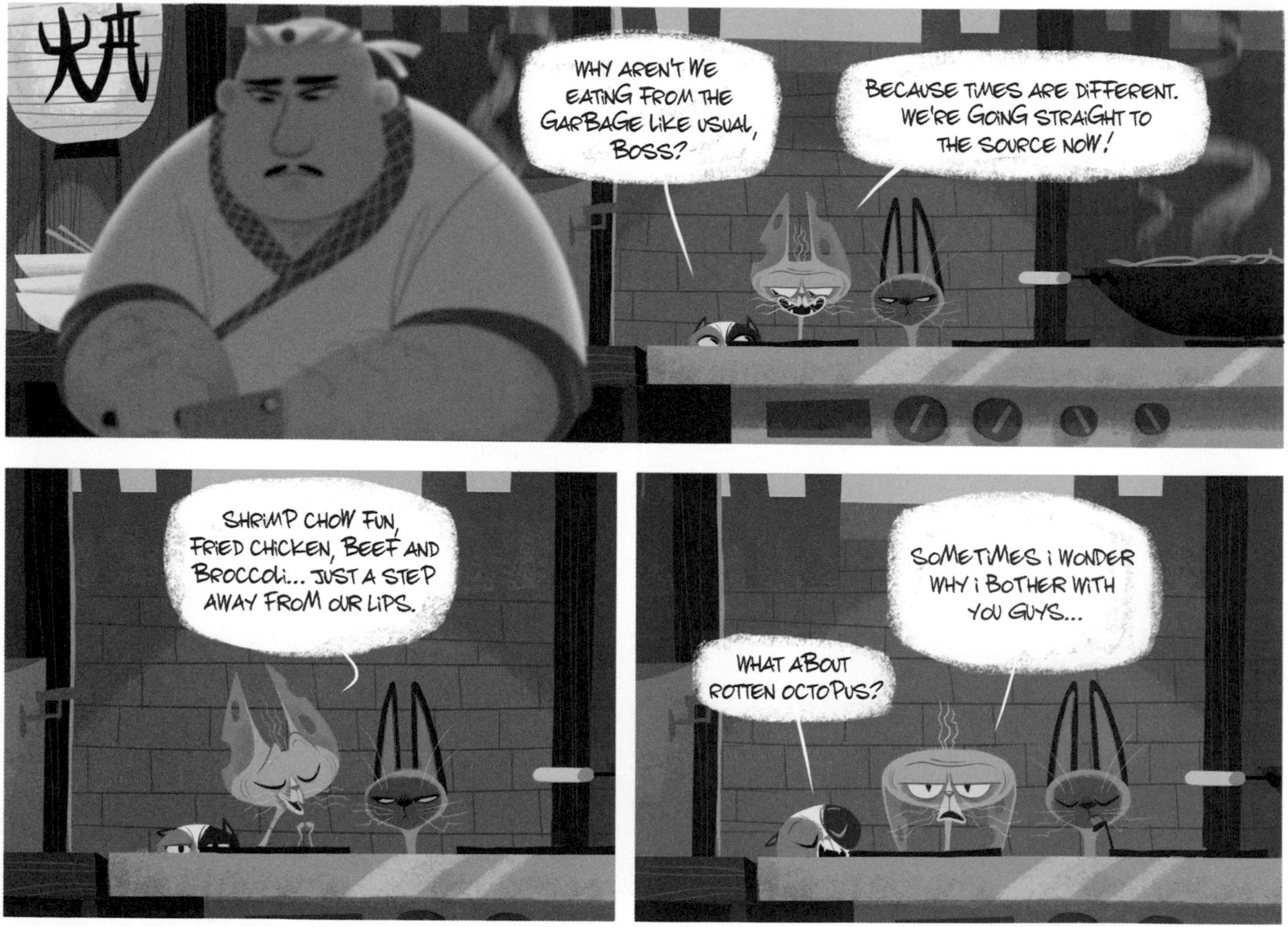
WHY AREN'T WE EATING FROM THE GARBAGE LIKE USUAL, BOSS?
BECAUSE TIMES ARE DIFFERENT. WE'RE GOING STRAIGHT TO THE SOURCE NOW!
SHRIMP CHOW FUN, FRIED CHICKEN, BEEF AND BROCCOLI... JUST A STEP AWAY FROM OUR LIPS.
SOMETIMES I WONDER WHY I BOTHER WITH YOU GUYS...
WHAT ABOUT ROTTEN OCTOPUS?

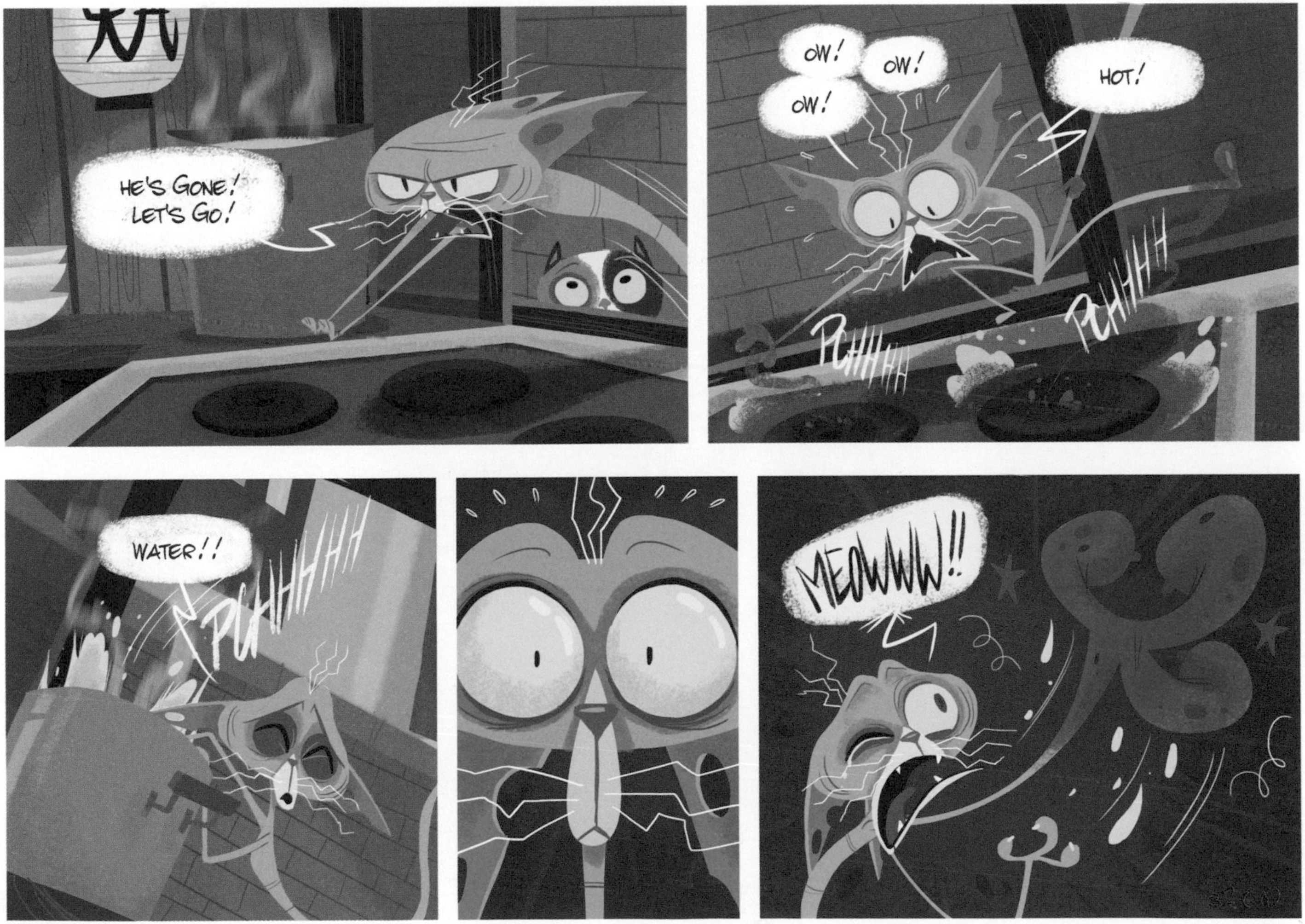
HE'S GONE!
LET'S GO!
OW!
OW!
OW!
HOT!
PCHHHHH
PCHHHHH
WATER!!
PCHHHHHH
MEOWWW!!

CONTINUED

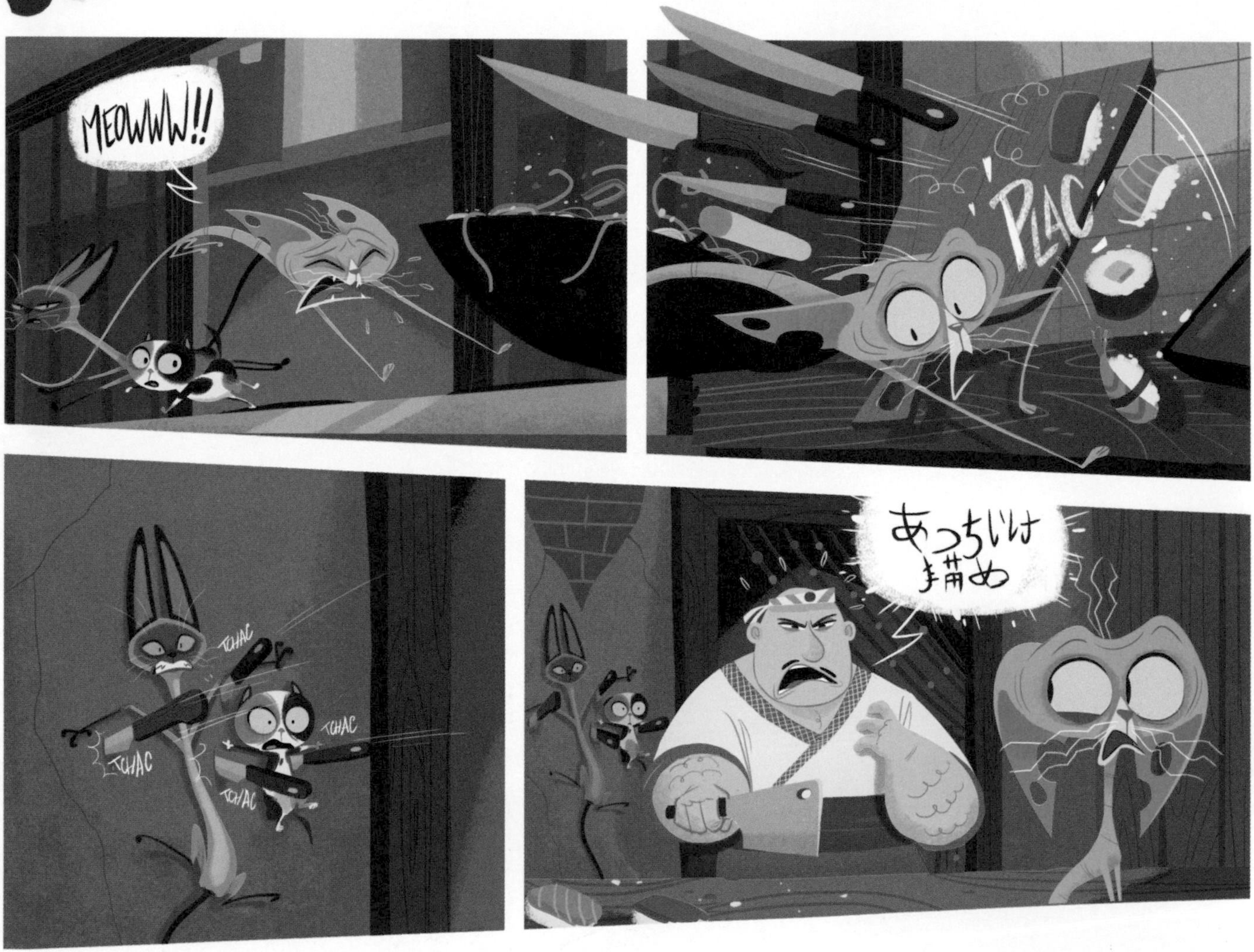
MEOWWW!!
PLAC
TCHAC
TCHAC
TCHAC
TCHAC
あっちいけ
猫め

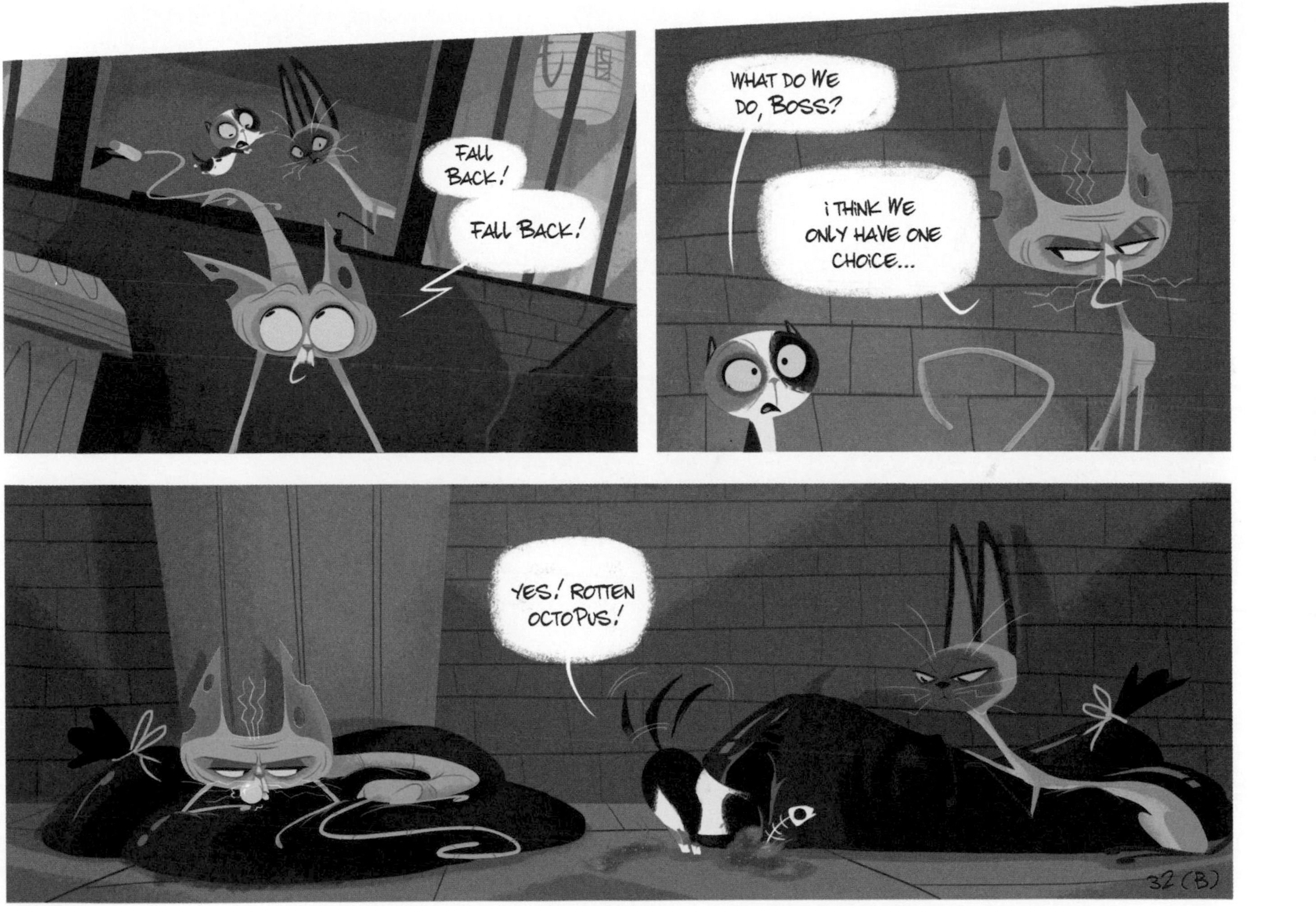

FALL BACK!
FALL BACK!
WHAT DO WE DO, BOSS?
I THINK WE ONLY HAVE ONE CHOICE...
YES! ROTTEN OCTOPUS!
32 (B)

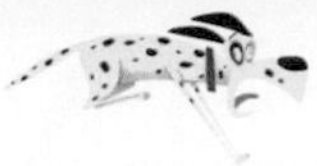

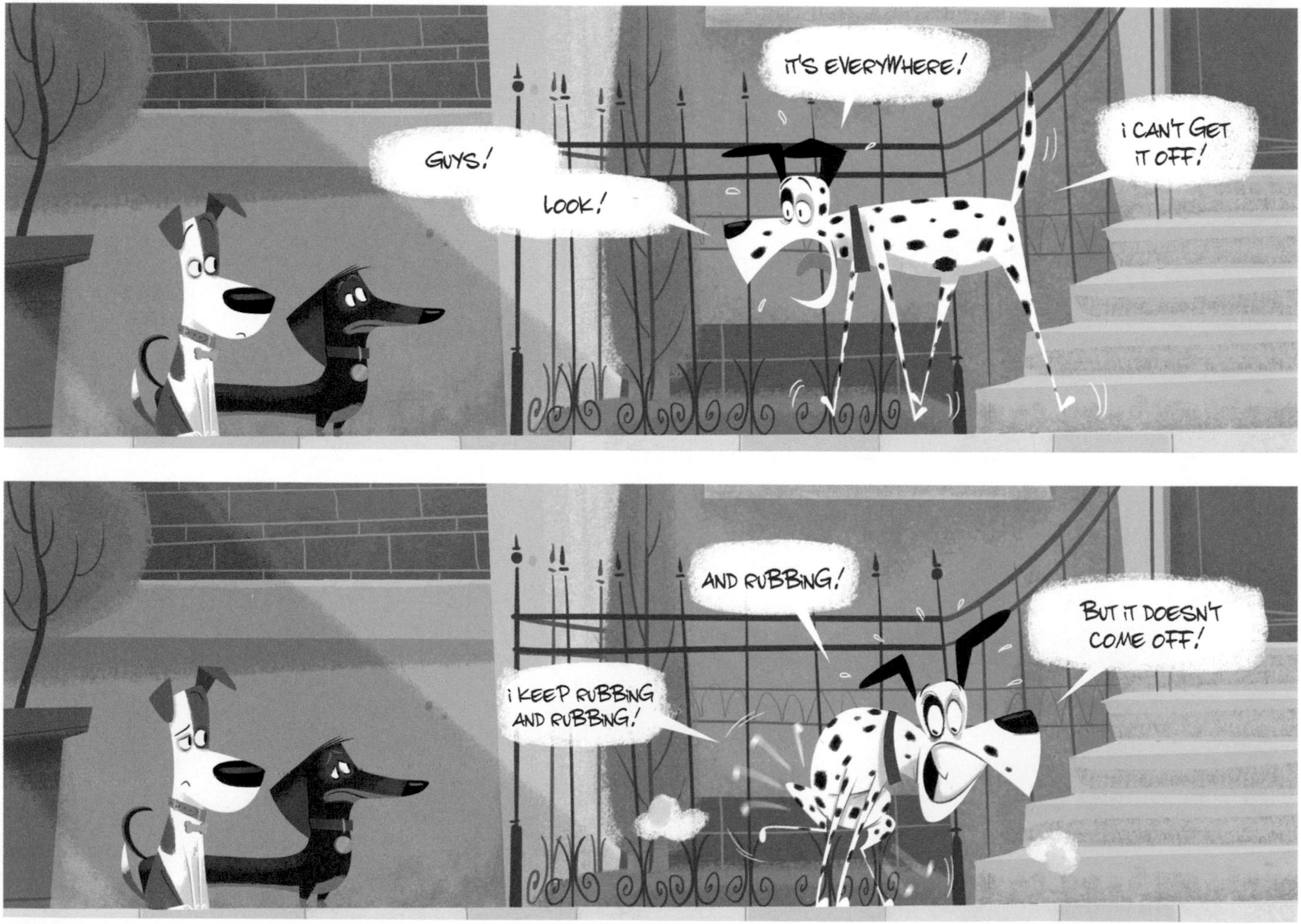
GUYS!
LOOK!
IT'S EVERYWHERE!
I CAN'T GET IT OFF!
I KEEP RUBBING AND RUBBING!
AND RUBBING!
BUT IT DOESN'T COME OFF!

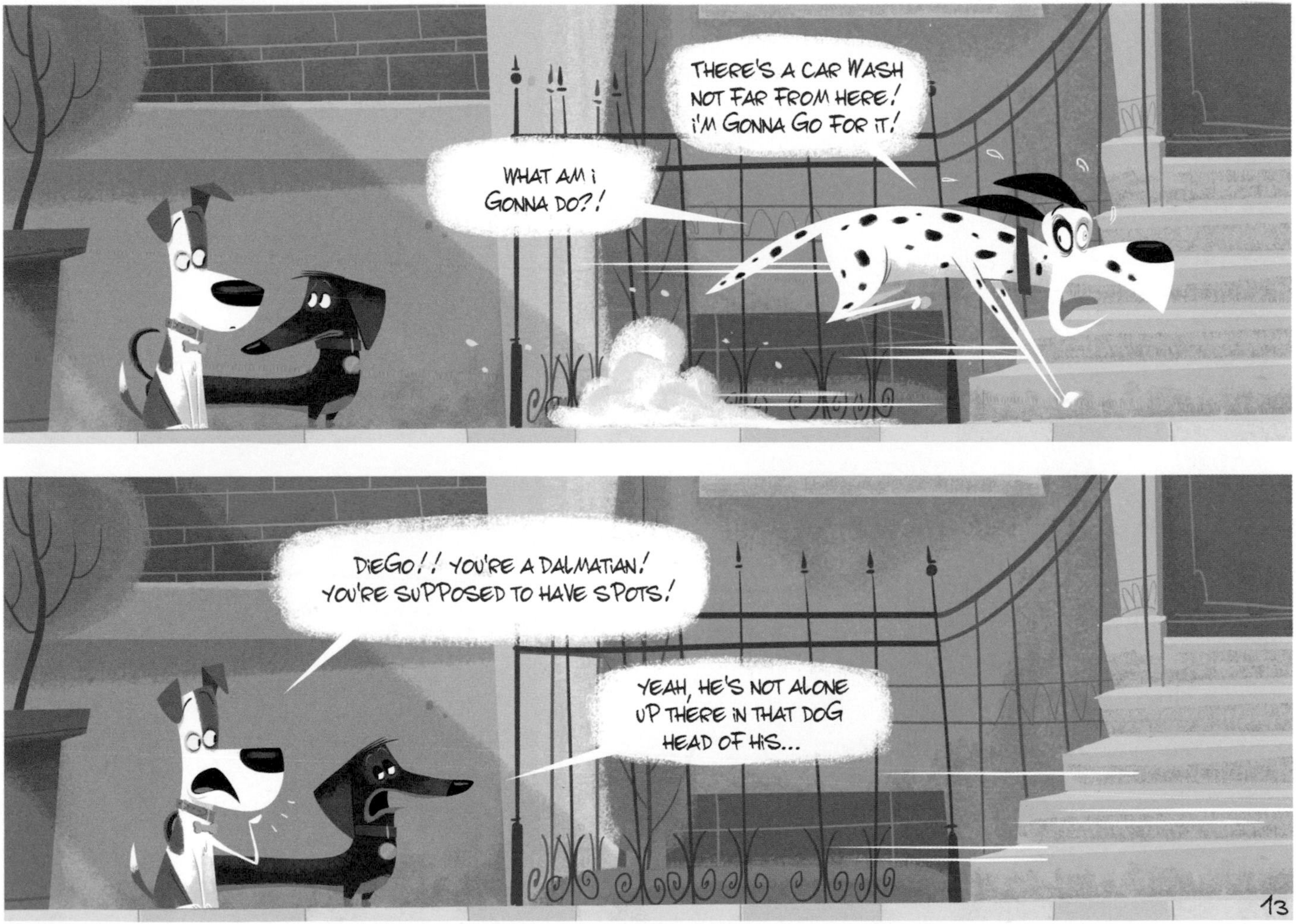
THERE'S A CAR WASH NOT FAR FROM HERE! I'M GONNA GO FOR IT!
WHAT AM I GONNA DO?!
DIEGO!! YOU'RE A DALMATIAN! YOU'RE SUPPOSED TO HAVE SPOTS!
YEAH, HE'S NOT ALONE UP THERE IN THAT DOG HEAD OF HIS...

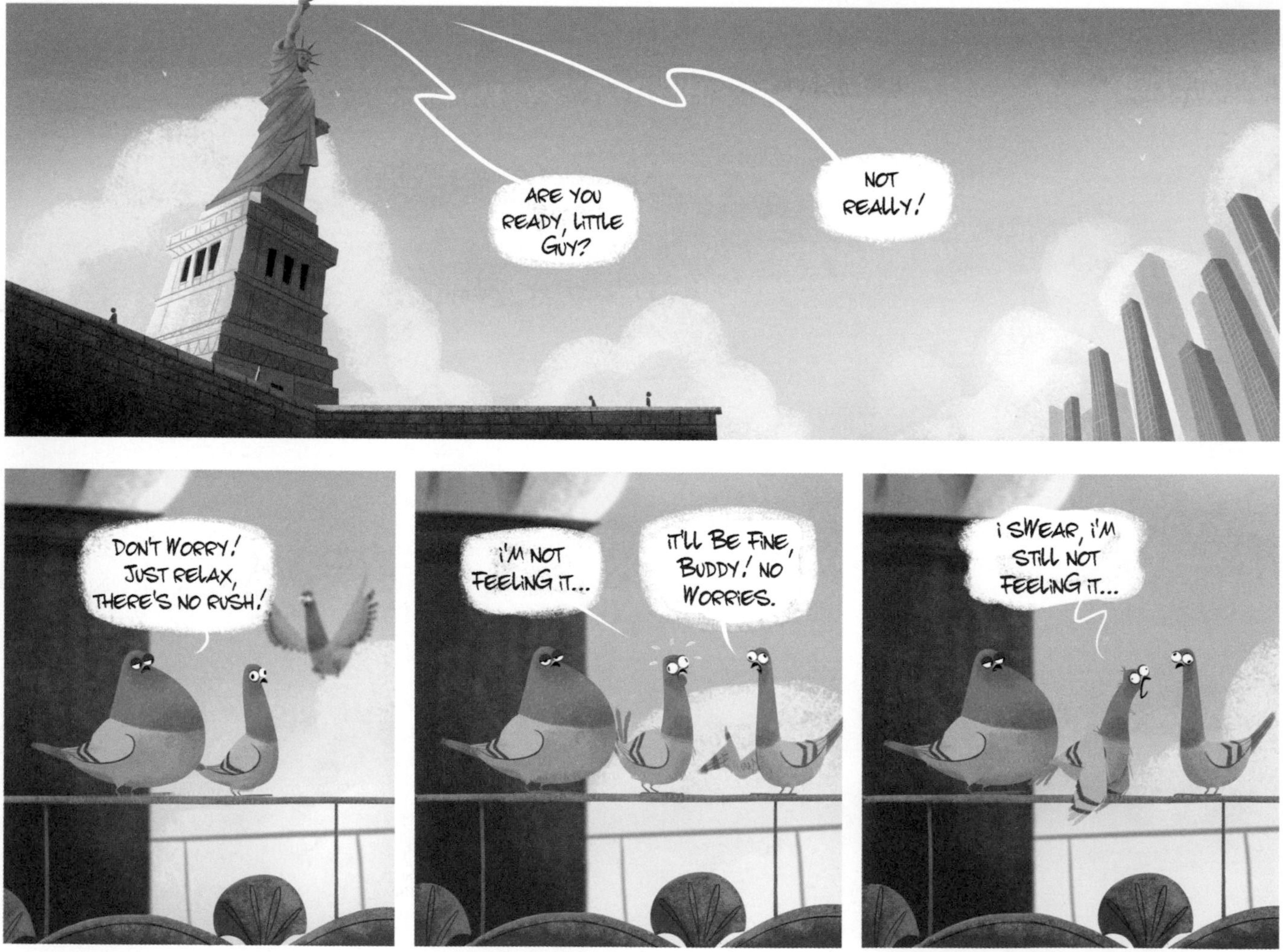
ARE YOU READY, LITTLE GUY?
NOT REALLY!
DON'T WORRY! JUST RELAX, THERE'S NO RUSH!
I'M NOT FEELING IT...
IT'LL BE FINE, BUDDY! NO WORRIES.
I SWEAR, I'M STILL NOT FEELING IT...

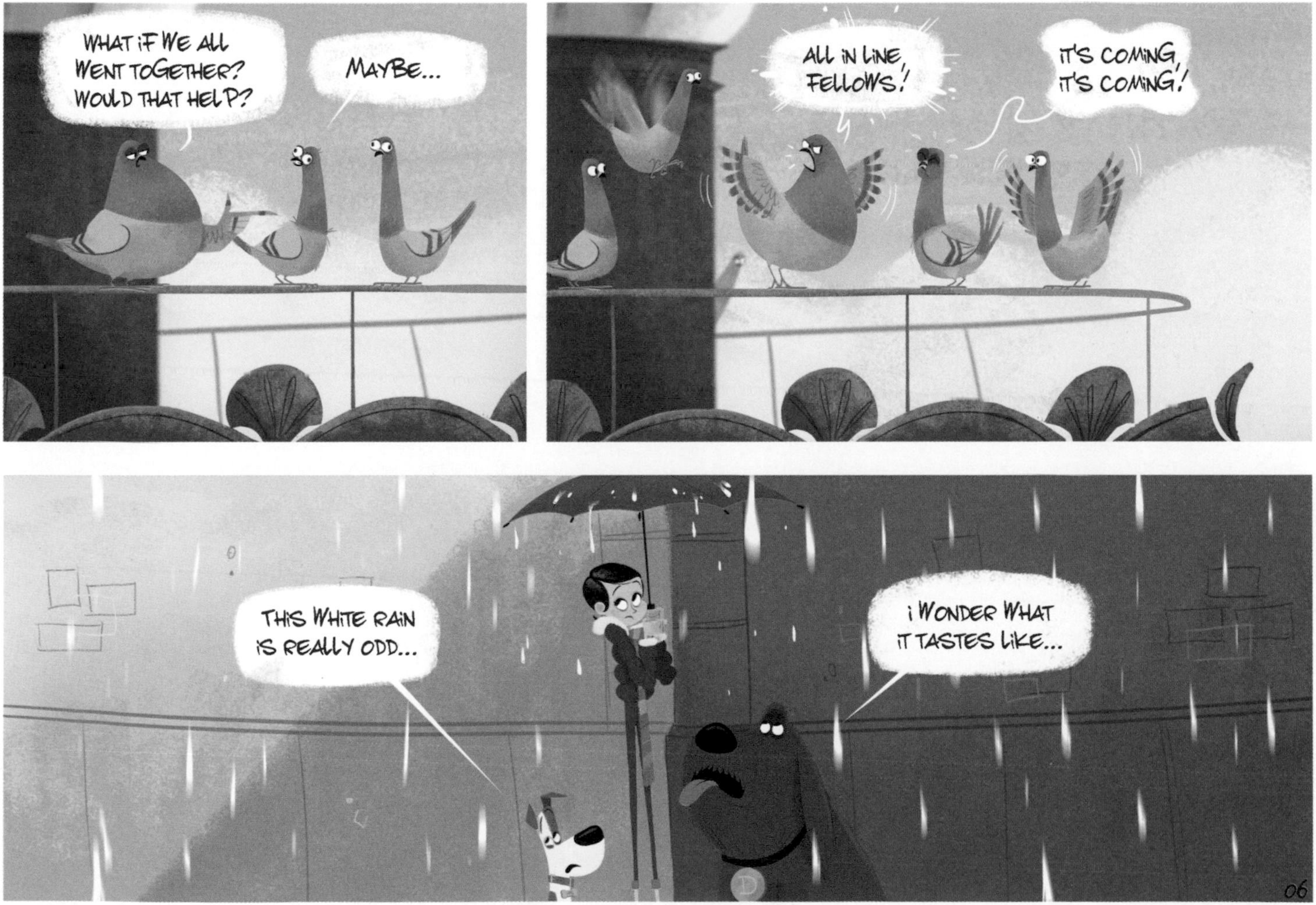
WHAT IF WE ALL WENT TOGETHER? WOULD THAT HELP?
MAYBE...
ALL IN LINE, FELLOWS!
IT'S COMING, IT'S COMING!
THIS WHITE RAIN IS REALLY ODD...
I WONDER WHAT IT TASTES LIKE...

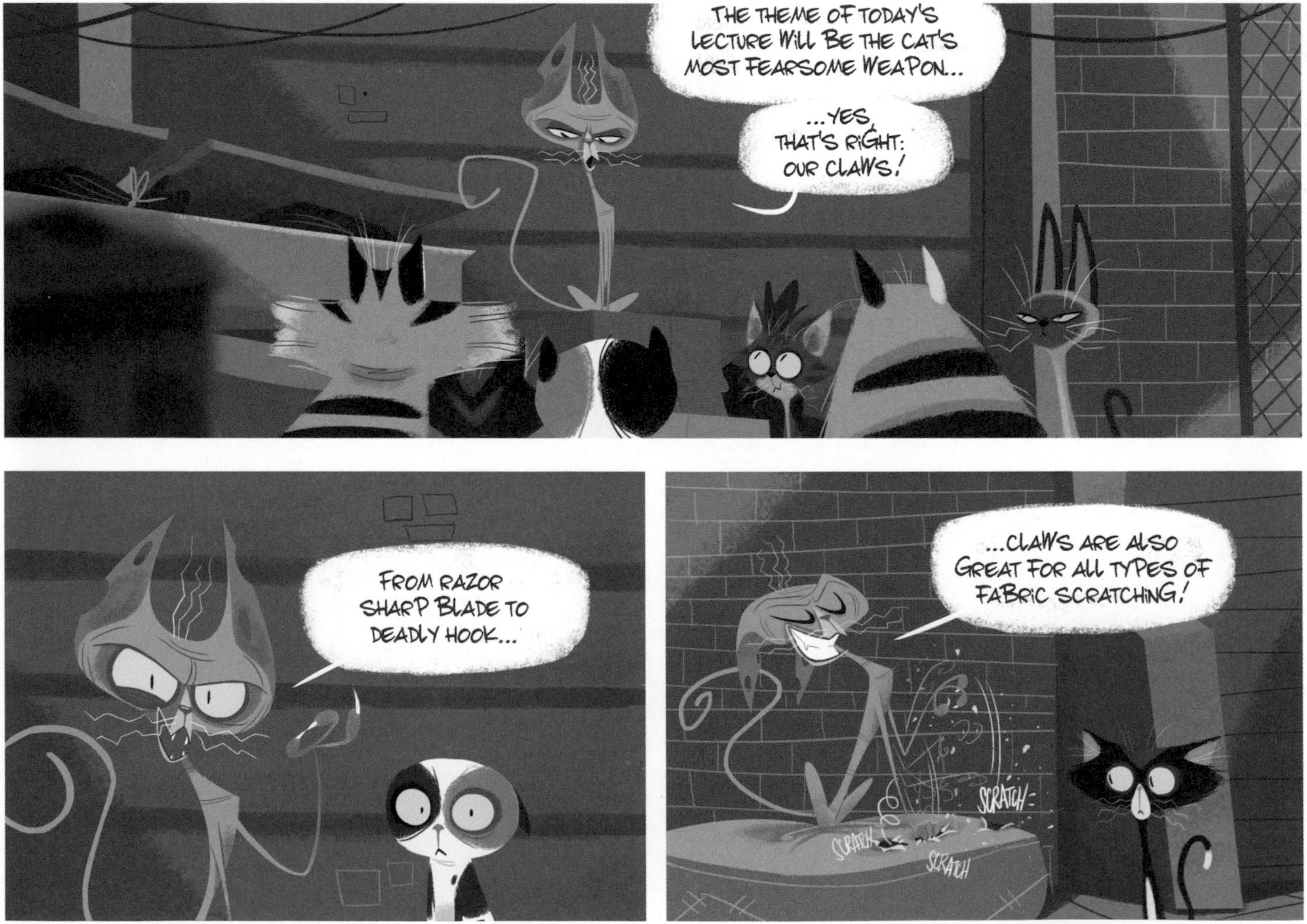
THE THEME OF TODAY'S LECTURE WILL BE THE CAT'S MOST FEARSOME WEAPON...
...YES, THAT'S RIGHT: OUR CLAWS!
FROM RAZOR SHARP BLADE TO DEADLY HOOK...
...CLAWS ARE ALSO GREAT FOR ALL TYPES OF FABRIC SCRATCHING!
SCRATCH!
SCRATCH
SCRATCH

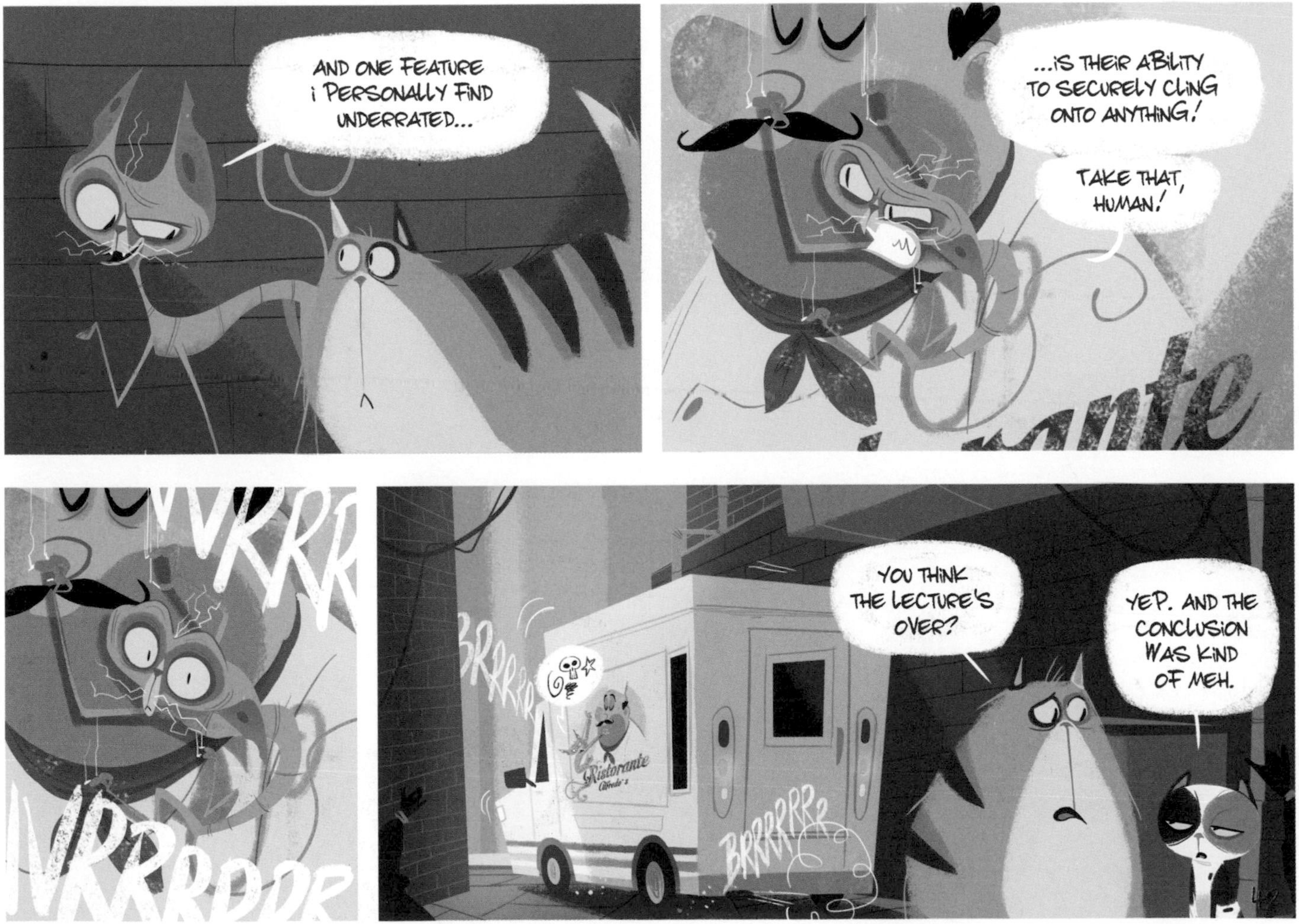
AND ONE FEATURE I PERSONALLY FIND UNDERRATED...
...IS THEIR ABILITY TO SECURELY CLING ONTO ANYTHING!
TAKE THAT, HUMAN!
YOU THINK THE LECTURE'S OVER?
YEP. AND THE CONCLUSION WAS KIND OF MEH.

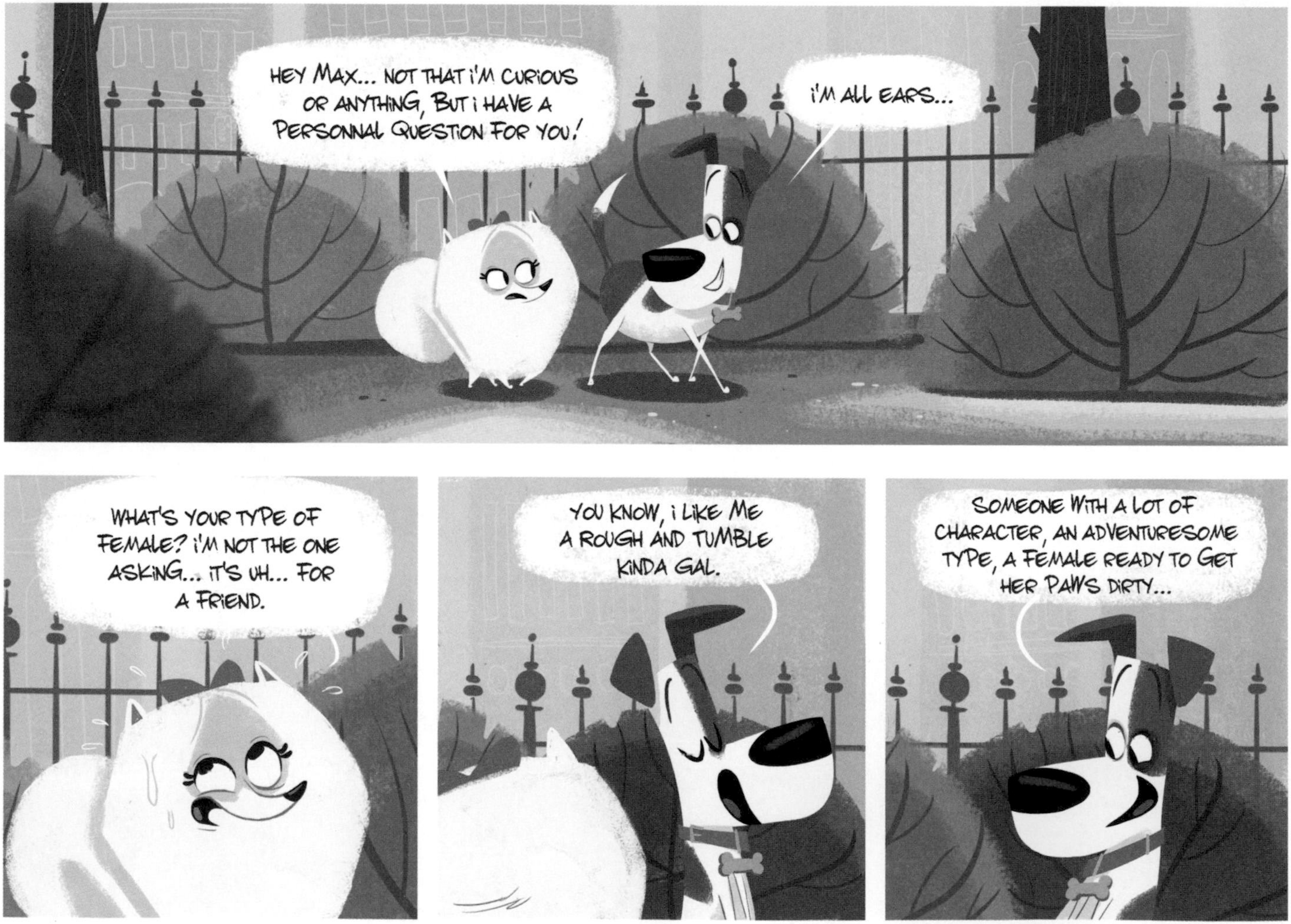
HEY MAX... NOT THAT i'M CURIOUS OR ANYTHING, BUT i HAVE A PERSONNAL QUESTION FOR YOU!
i'M ALL EARS...
WHAT'S YOUR TYPE OF FEMALE? i'M NOT THE ONE ASKING... IT'S UH... FOR A FRIEND.
YOU KNOW, i LIKE ME A ROUGH AND TUMBLE KINDA GAL.
SOMEONE WITH A LOT OF CHARACTER, AN ADVENTURESOME TYPE, A FEMALE READY TO GET HER PAWS DIRTY...

22

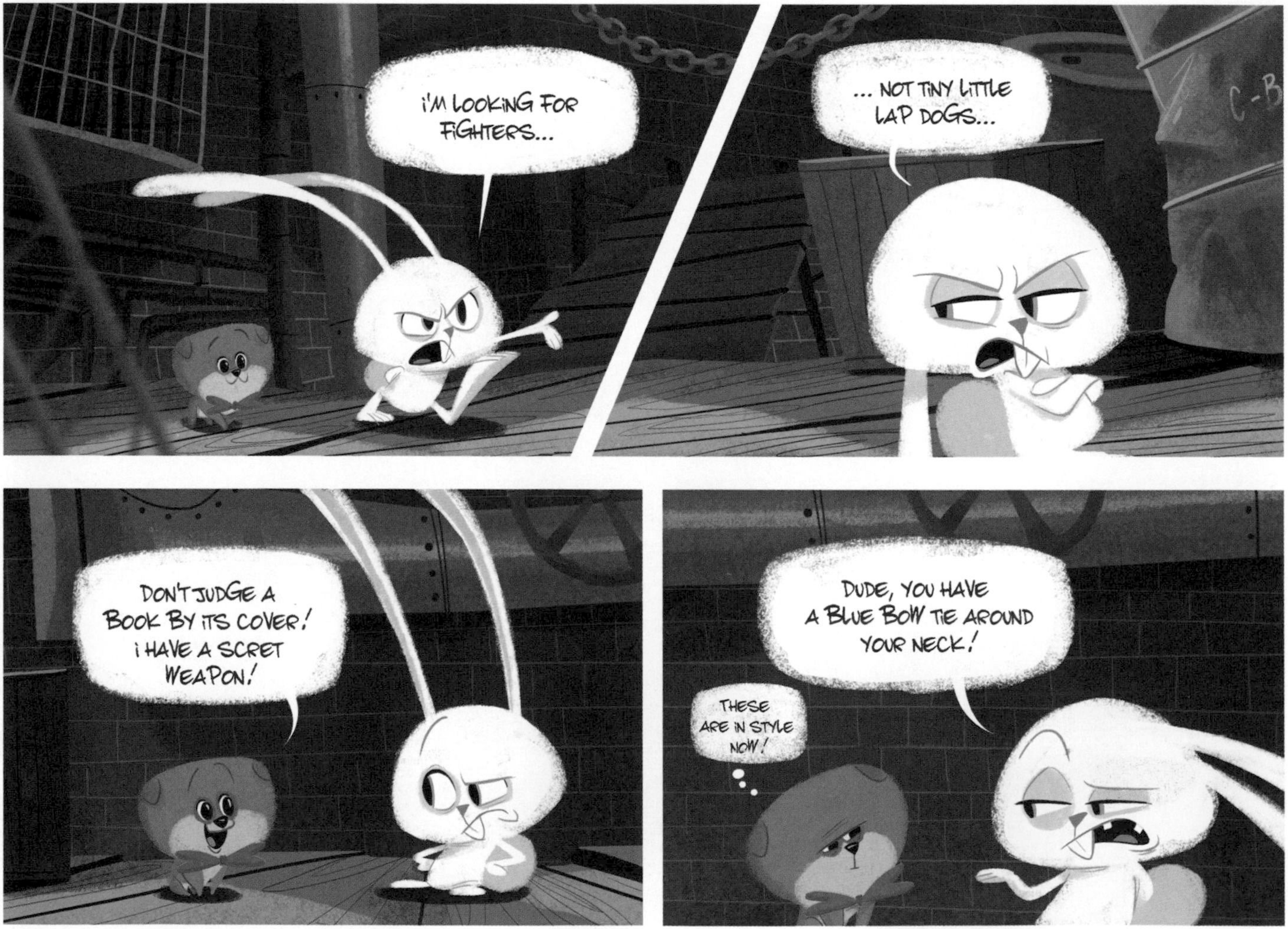
I'M LOOKING FOR FIGHTERS...
... NOT TINY LITTLE LAP DOGS...
C-B
DON'T JUDGE A BOOK BY ITS COVER! I HAVE A SCRET WEAPON!
DUDE, YOU HAVE A BLUE BOW TIE AROUND YOUR NECK!
THESE ARE IN STYLE NOW!

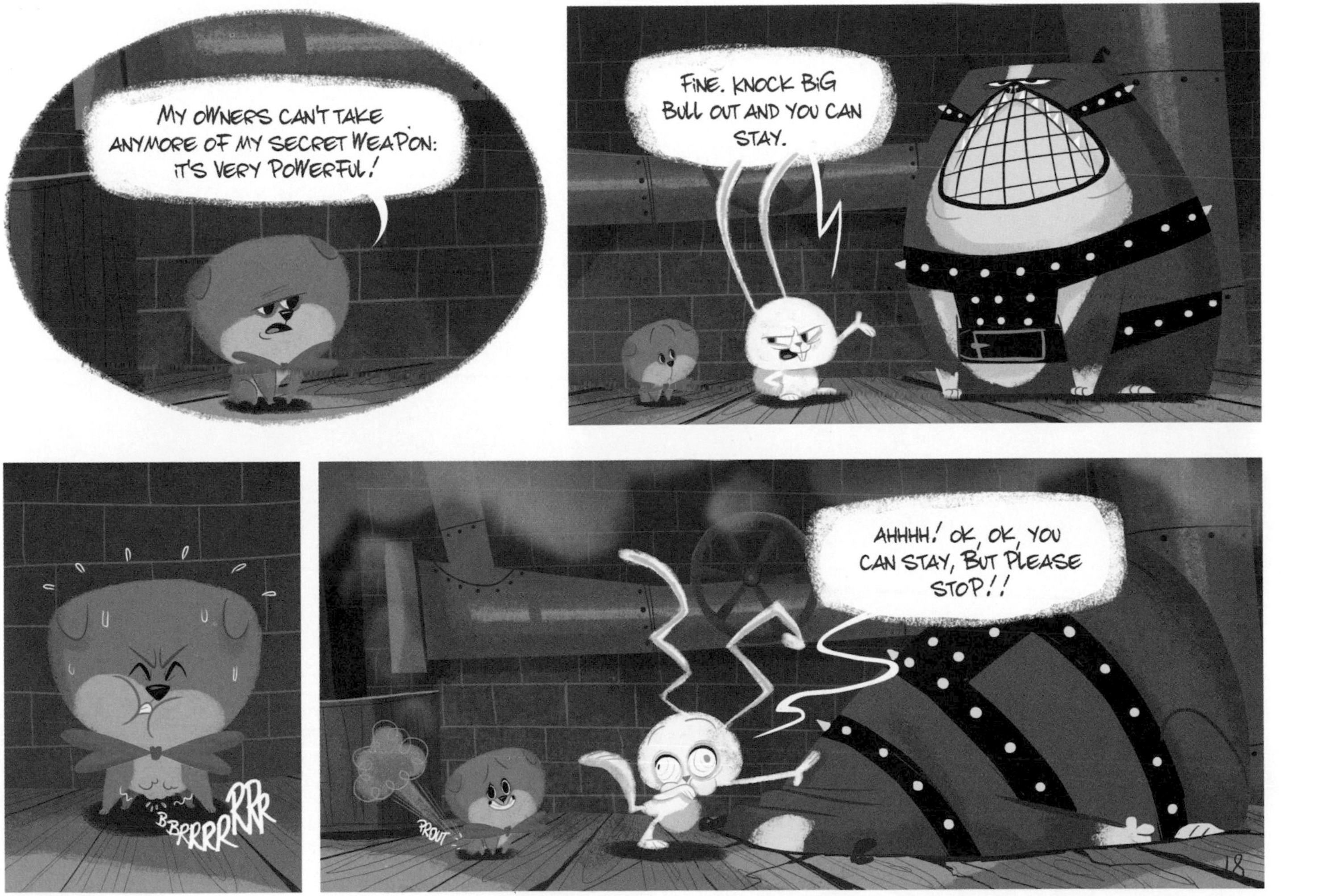

MY OWNERS CAN'T TAKE ANYMORE OF MY SECRET WEAPON: IT'S VERY POWERFUL!
FINE. KNOCK BIG BULL OUT AND YOU CAN STAY.
BBRRRRRRR
PROUT
AHHHH! OK, OK, YOU CAN STAY, BUT PLEASE STOP!!

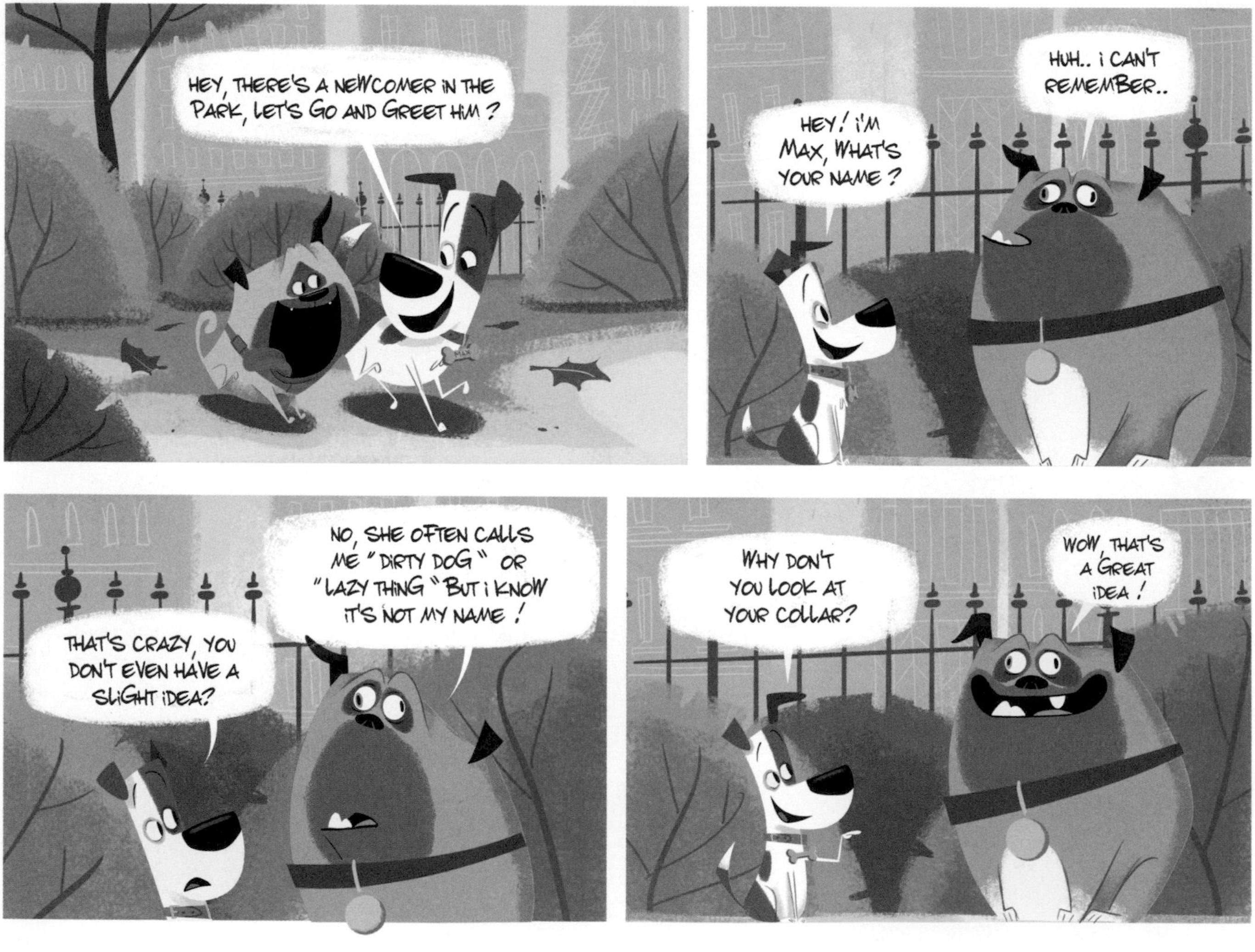
HEY, THERE'S A NEWCOMER IN THE PARK, LET'S GO AND GREET HIM ?
HEY ! I'M MAX, WHAT'S YOUR NAME ?
HUH.. I CAN'T REMEMBER..
THAT'S CRAZY, YOU DON'T EVEN HAVE A SLIGHT IDEA?
NO, SHE OFTEN CALLS ME " DIRTY DOG " OR " LAZY THING " BUT I KNOW IT'S NOT MY NAME !
WHY DON'T YOU LOOK AT YOUR COLLAR?
WOW, THAT'S A GREAT IDEA !

03

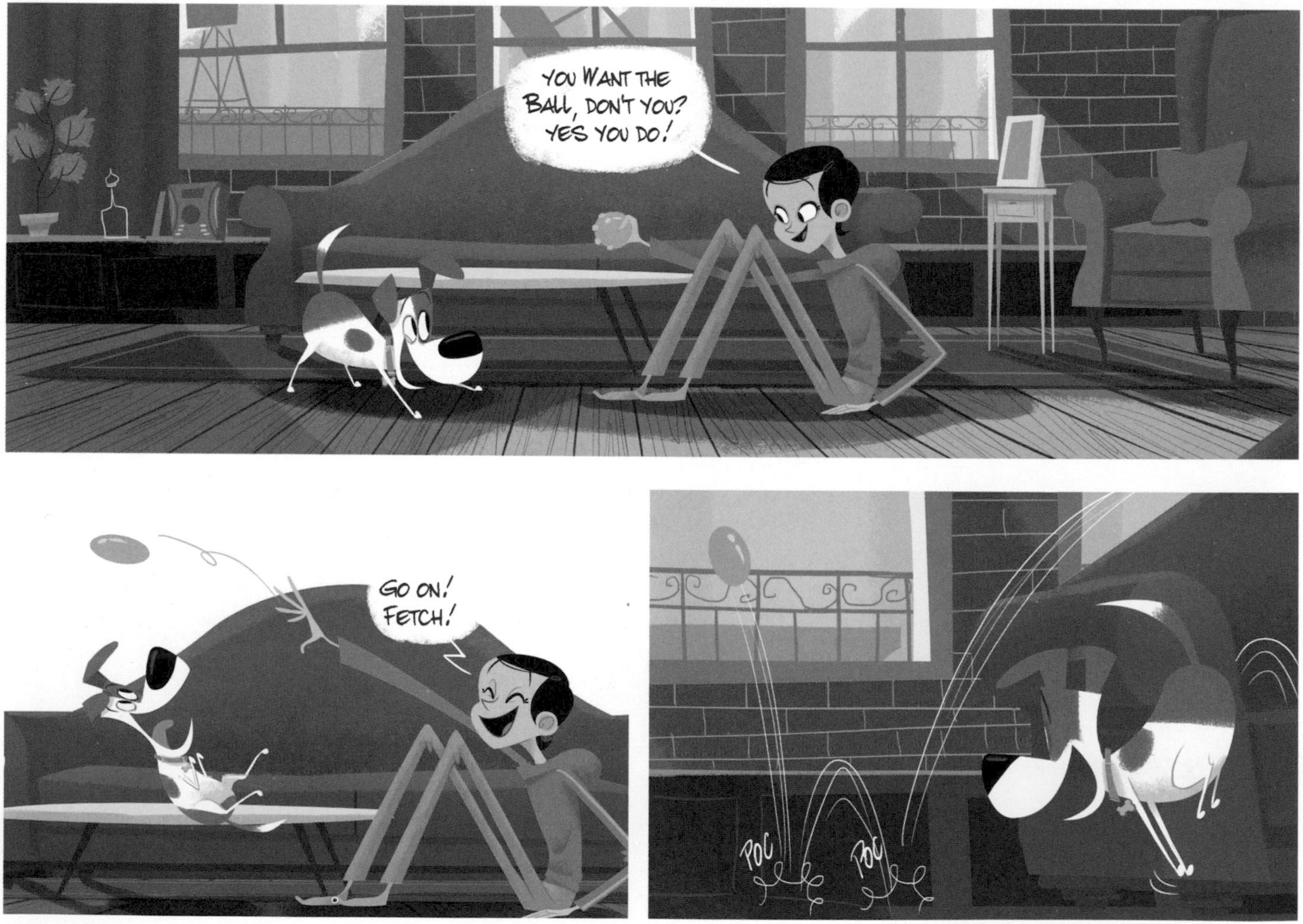
YOU WANT THE BALL, DON'T YOU? YES YOU DO!
GO ON! FETCH!
POC
POC

41

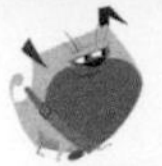

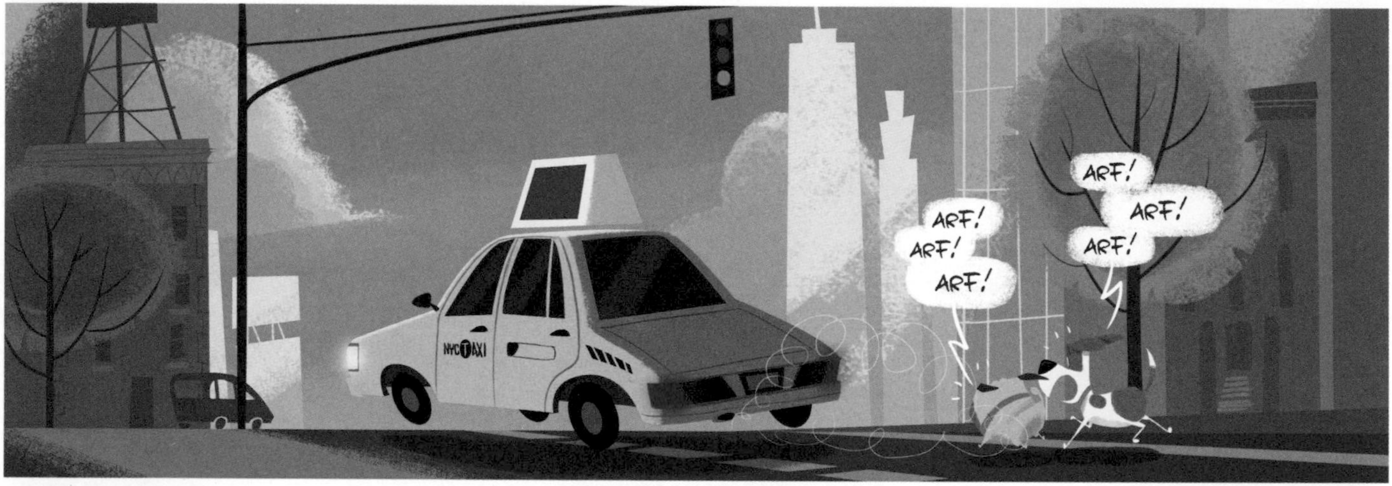
ARF!
ARF!
ARF!
ARF!
ARF!
ARF!

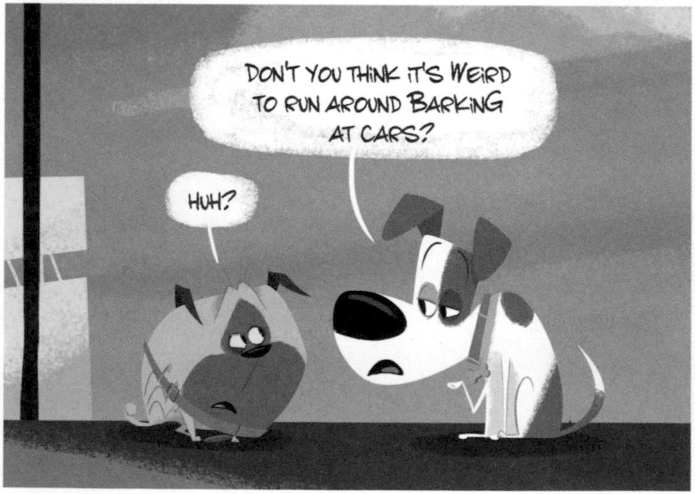
DON'T YOU THINK IT'S WEIRD TO RUN AROUND BARKING AT CARS?
HUH?

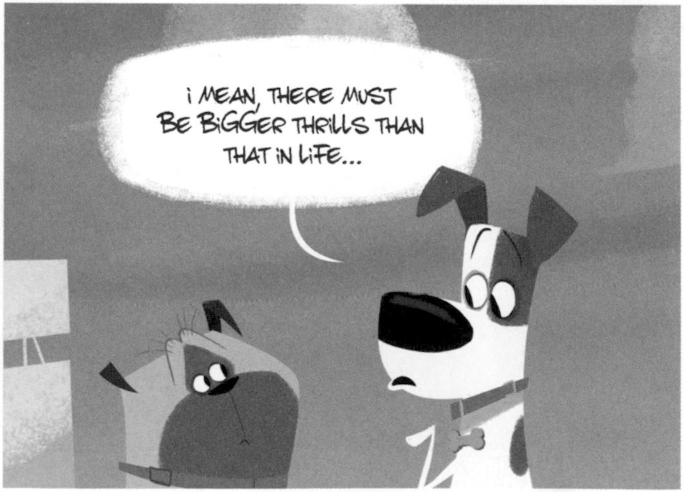
I MEAN, THERE MUST BE BIGGER THRILLS THAN THAT IN LIFE...

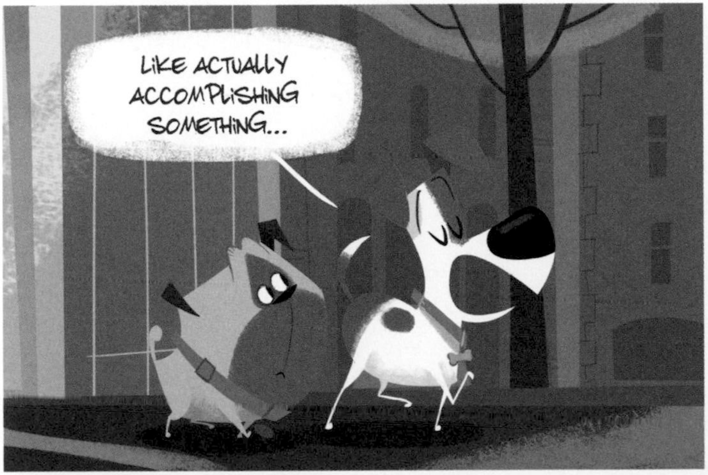
LIKE ACTUALLY ACCOMPLISHING SOMETHING...

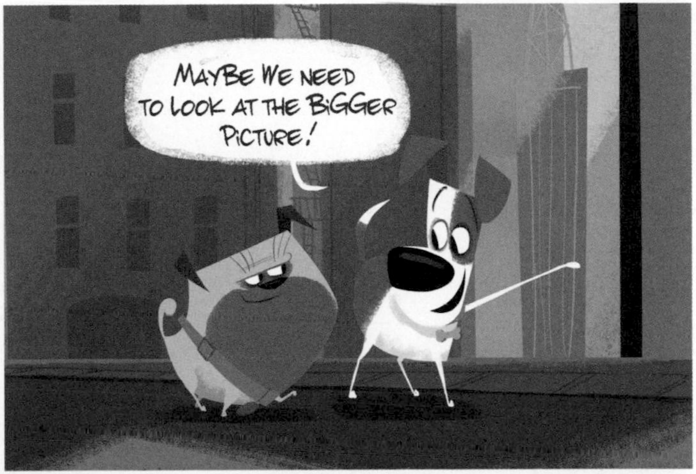
MAYBE WE NEED TO LOOK AT THE BIGGER PICTURE!

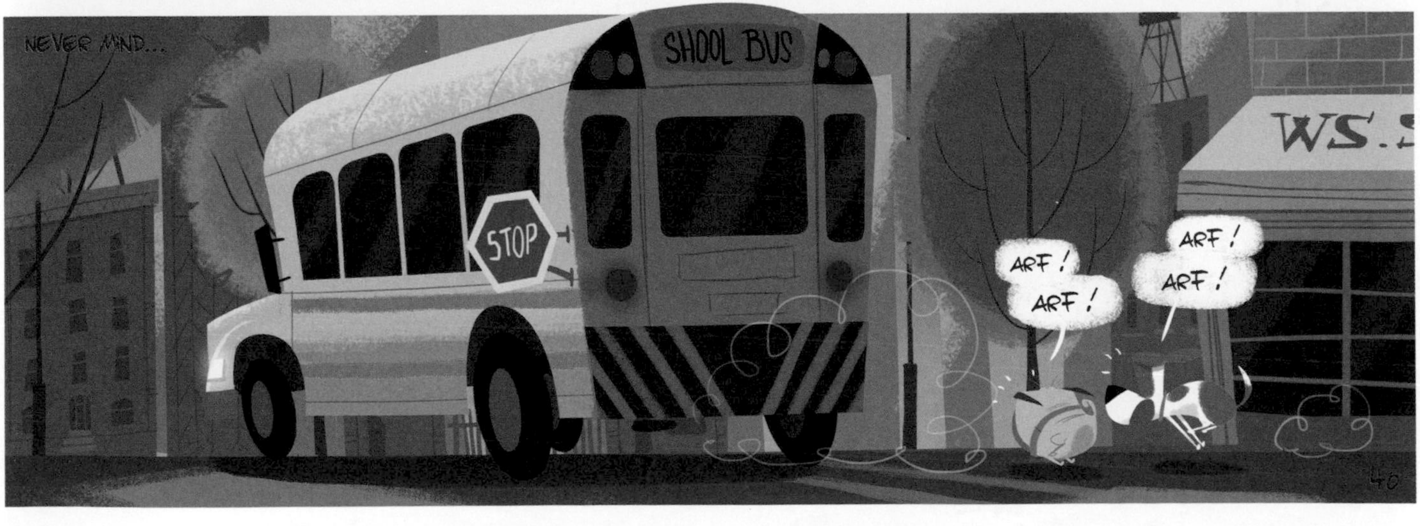
NEVER MIND...
SHOOL BUS
STOP
WS.
ARF!
ARF!
ARF!
ARF!

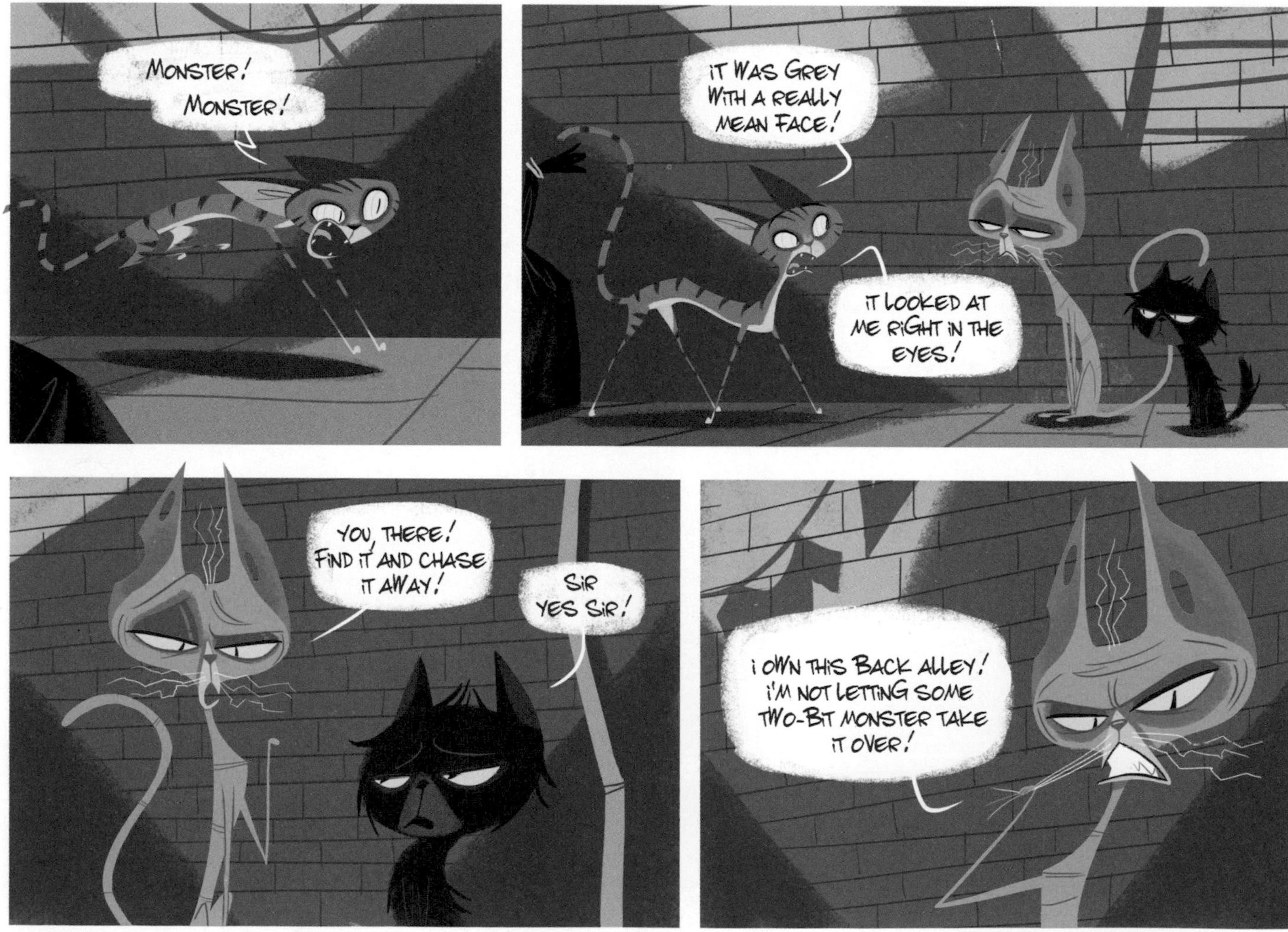
MONSTER!
MONSTER!
IT WAS GREY WITH A REALLY MEAN FACE!
IT LOOKED AT ME RIGHT IN THE EYES!
YOU, THERE! FIND IT AND CHASE IT AWAY!
SIR YES SIR!
I OWN THIS BACK ALLEY! I'M NOT LETTING SOME TWO-BIT MONSTER TAKE IT OVER!

47

44

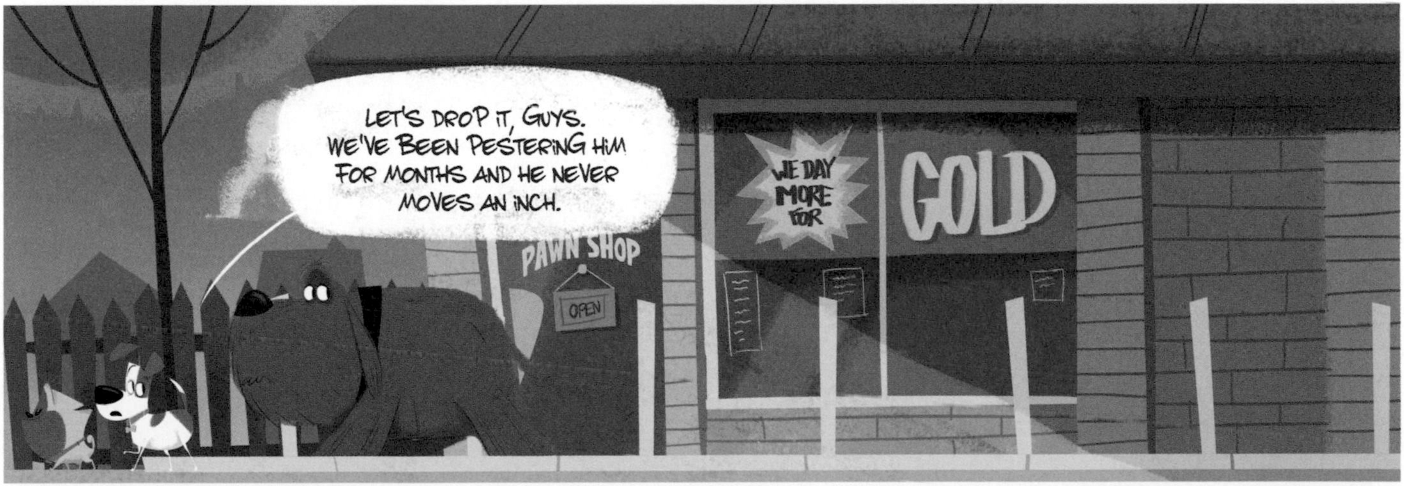
LET'S DROP IT, GUYS. WE'VE BEEN PESTERING HIM FOR MONTHS AND HE NEVER MOVES AN INCH.
WE DAY MORE FOR
GOLD
PAWN SHOP
OPEN

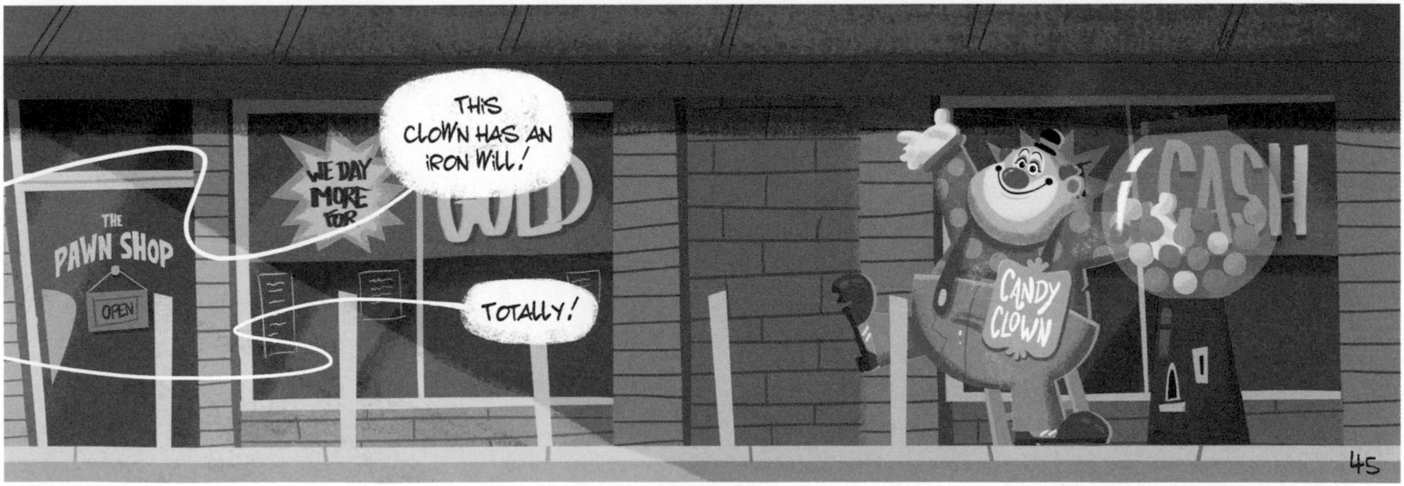
THIS CLOWN HAS AN IRON WILL!
TOTALLY!
THE PAWN SHOP
OPEN
WE DAY MORE FOR
CASH
CANDY CLOWN

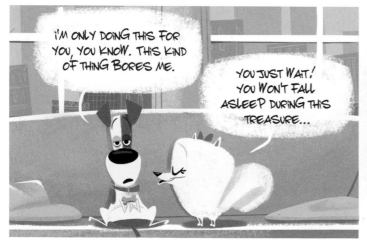

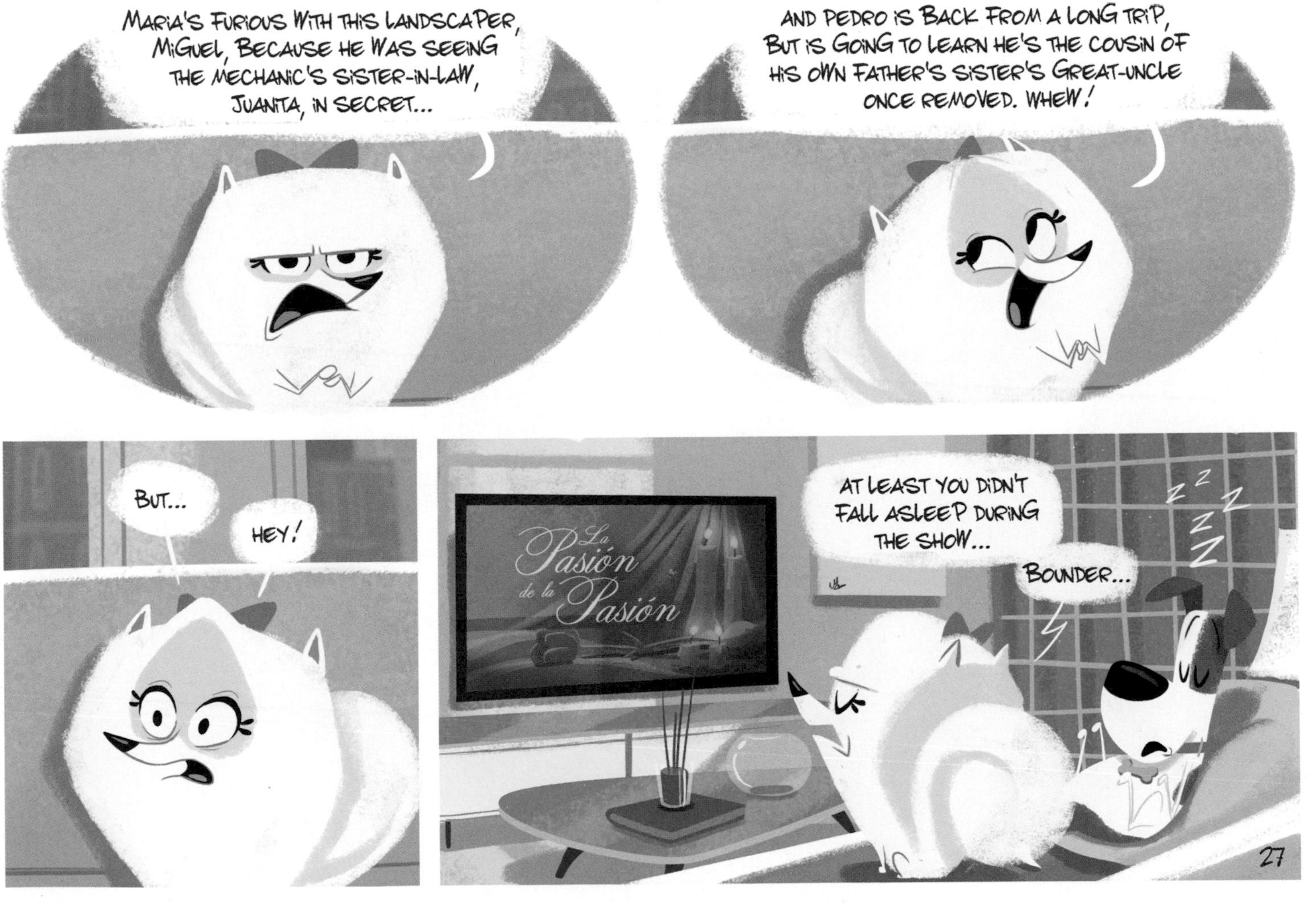
MARIA'S FURIOUS WITH THIS LANDSCAPER, MIGUEL, BECAUSE HE WAS SEEING THE MECHANIC'S SISTER-IN-LAW, JUANITA, IN SECRET...
AND PEDRO IS BACK FROM A LONG TRIP, BUT IS GOING TO LEARN HE'S THE COUSIN OF HIS OWN FATHER'S SISTER'S GREAT-UNCLE ONCE REMOVED. WHEW!
BUT...
HEY!
La Pasión de la Pasión
AT LEAST YOU DIDN'T FALL ASLEEP DURING THE SHOW...
BOUNDER...
Z Z Z Z Z

07

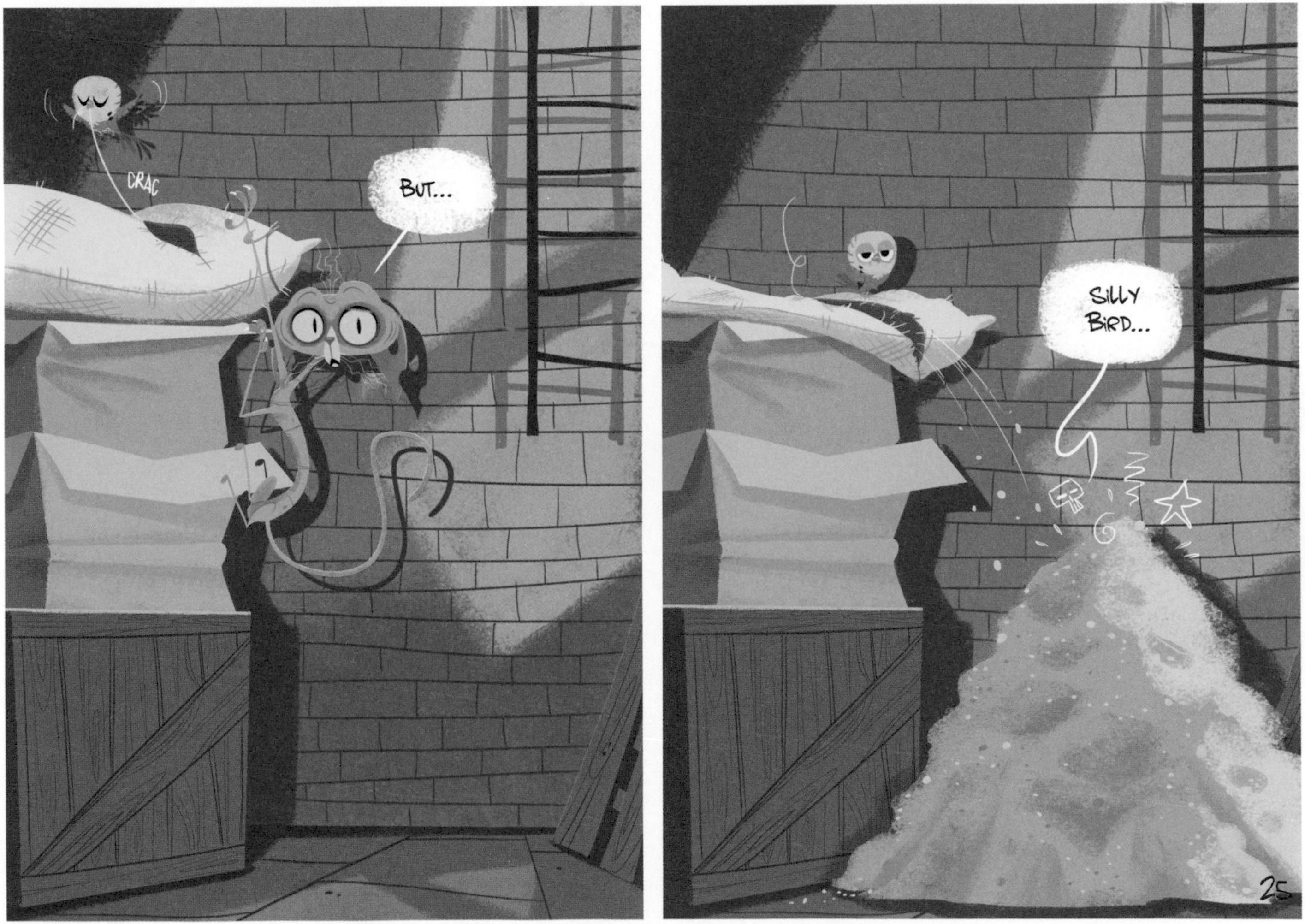
CRAC
BUT...
SILLY BIRD...

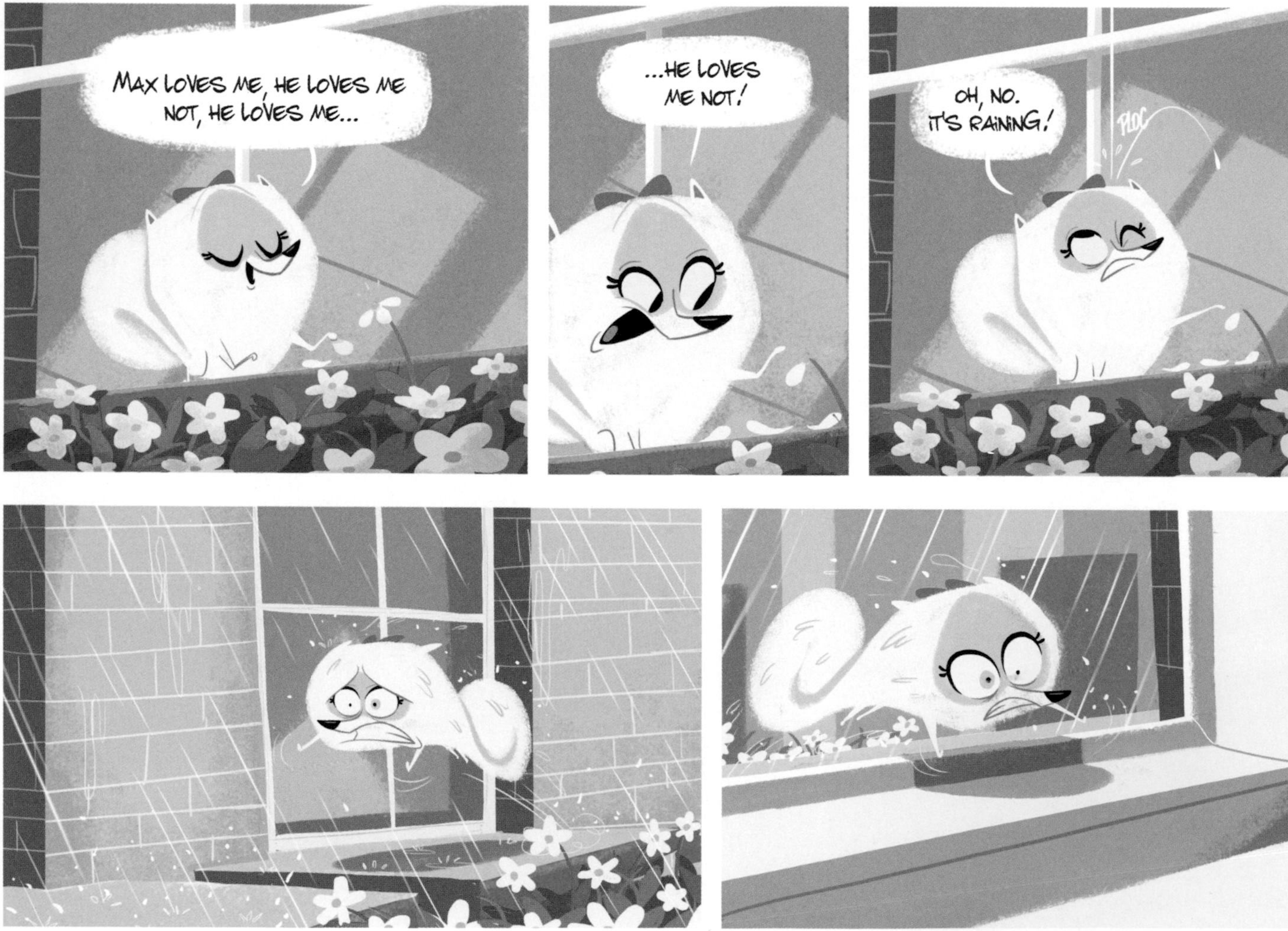
MAX LOVES ME, HE LOVES ME NOT, HE LOVES ME...
...HE LOVES ME NOT!
OH, NO. IT'S RAINING!
PLOC

36

19

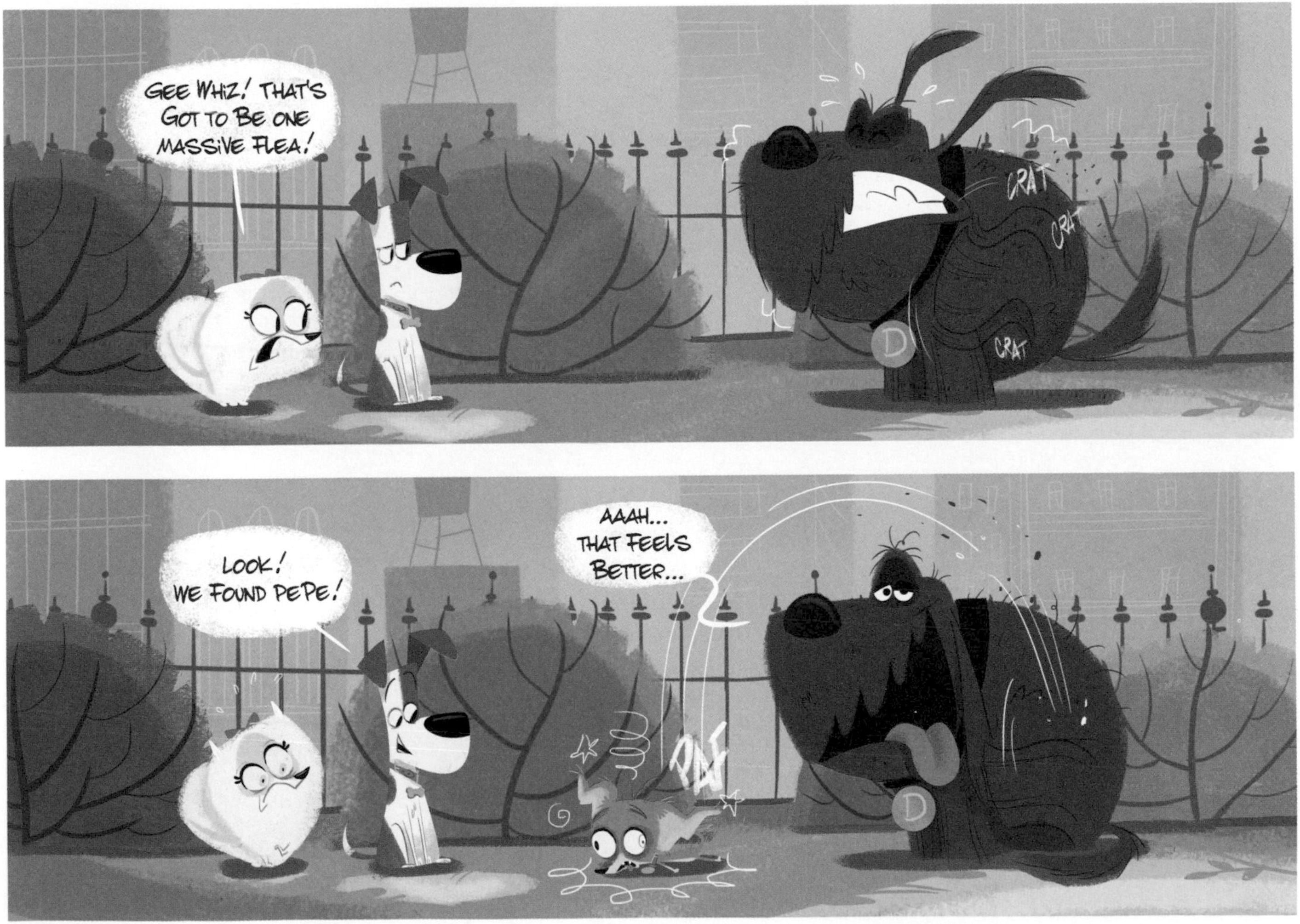
GEE WHIZ! THAT'S GOT TO BE ONE MASSIVE FLEA!
CRAT
CRAT
CRAT
LOOK! WE FOUND PEPE!
AAAH... THAT FEELS BETTER...
PAF

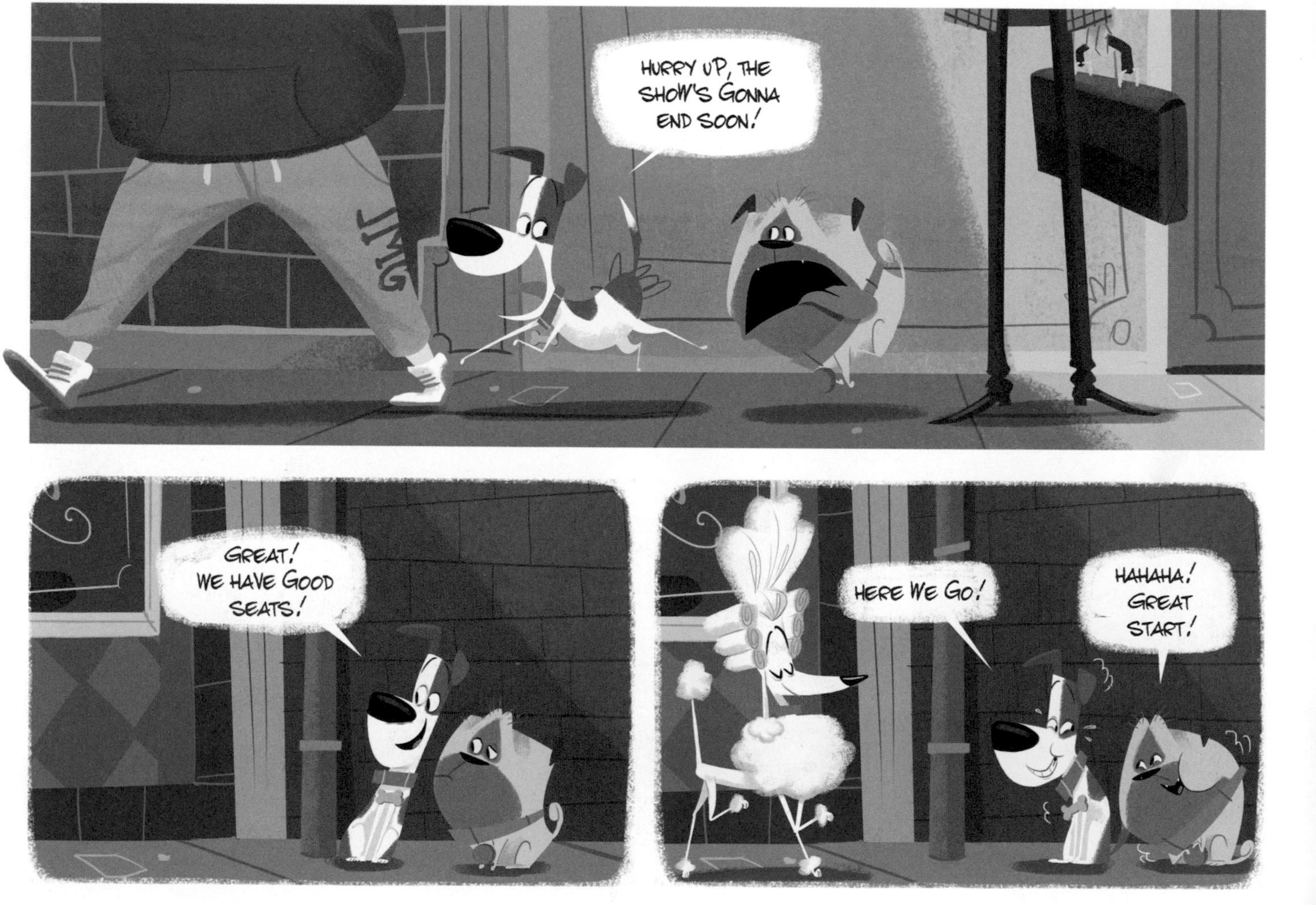
HURRY UP, THE SHOW'S GONNA END SOON!
GREAT! WE HAVE GOOD SEATS!
HERE WE GO!
HAHAHA! GREAT START!

16

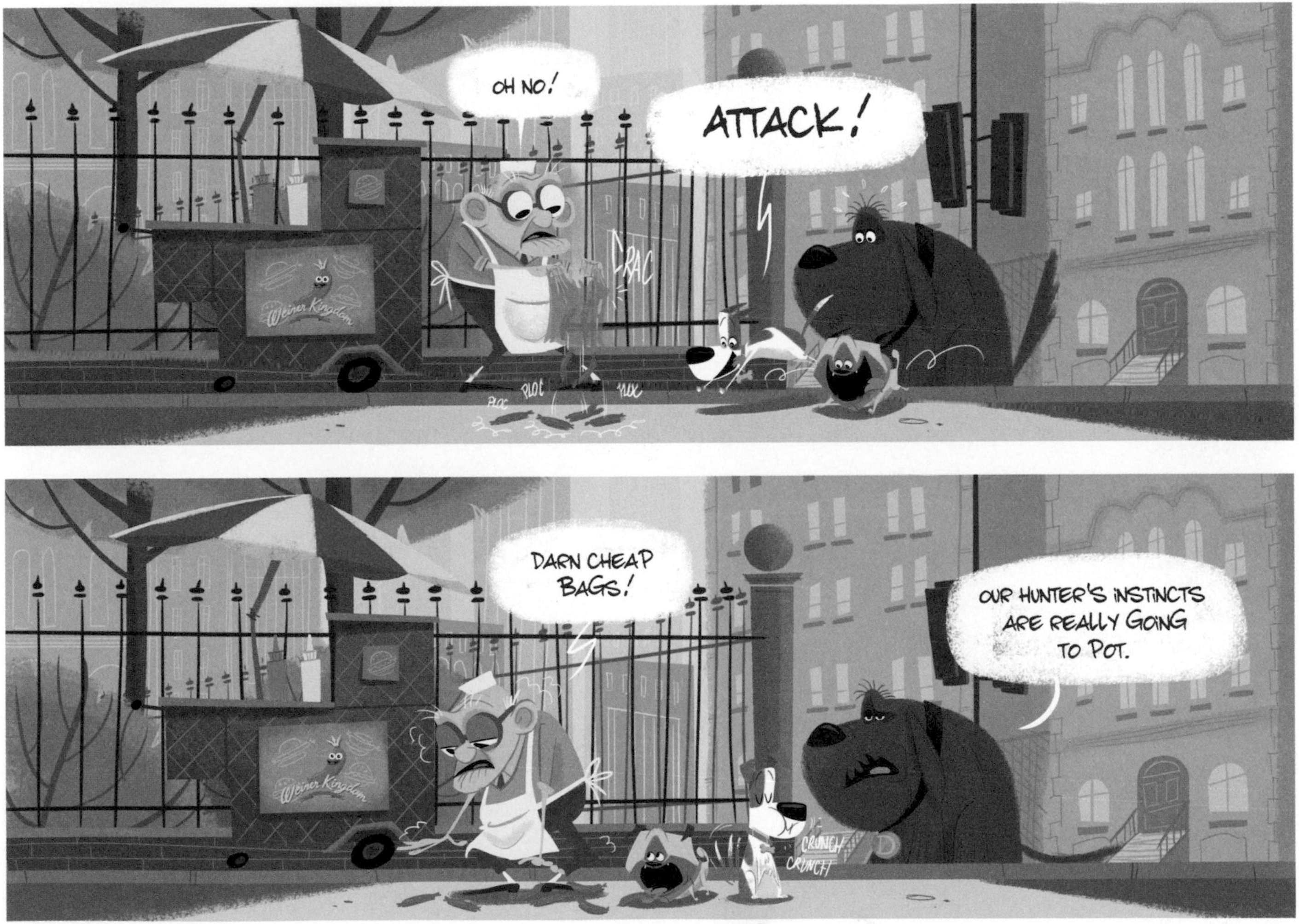
Weiner Kingdom
OH NO!
ATTACK!
CRAC
PLOC
PLOC
DARN CHEAP BAGS!
Weiner Kingdom
OUR HUNTER'S INSTINCTS ARE REALLY GOING TO POT.
CRUNCH
CRUNCH

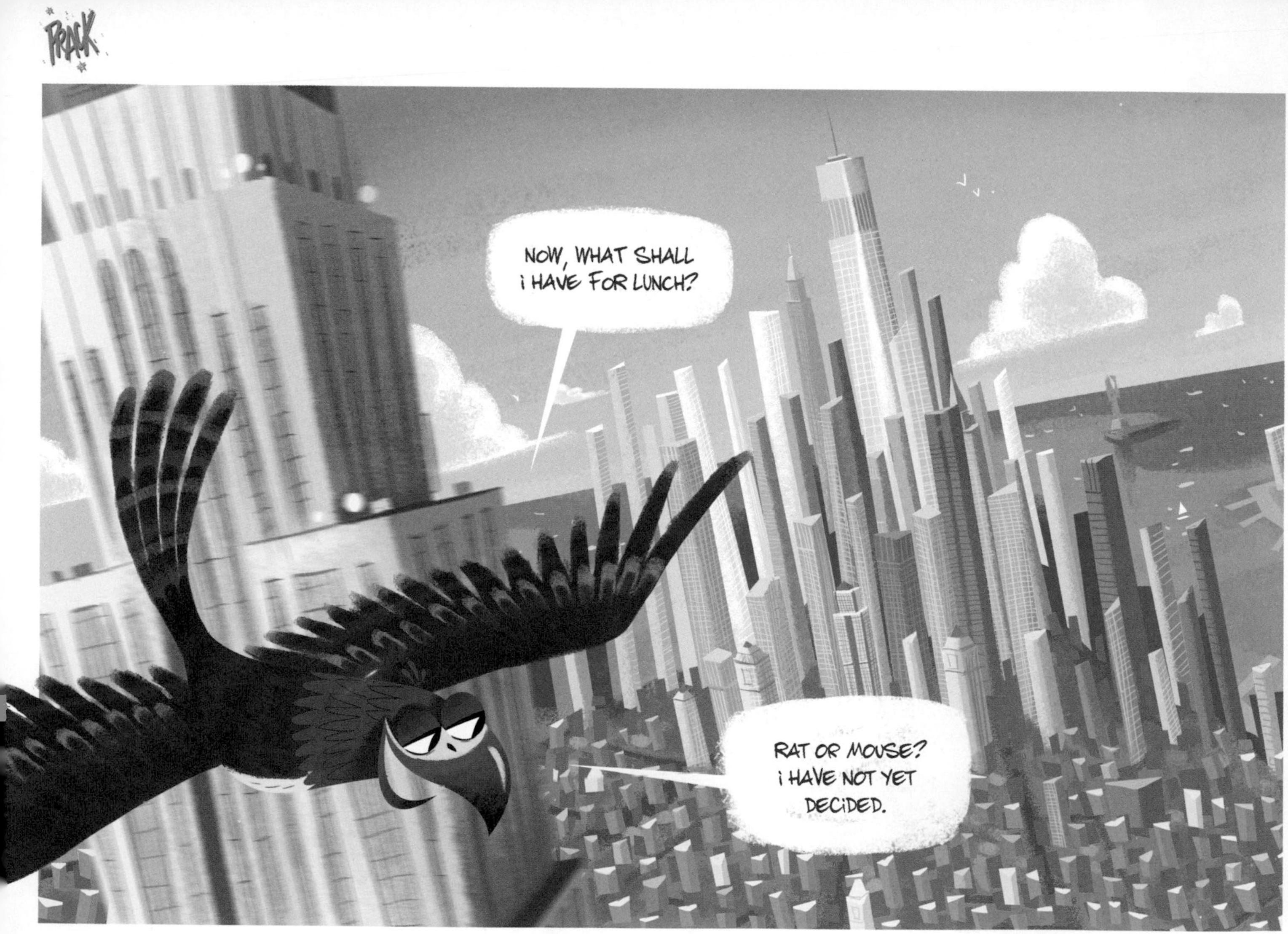
PRACK
NOW, WHAT SHALL I HAVE FOR LUNCH?
RAT OR MOUSE? I HAVE NOT YET DECIDED.

09

39

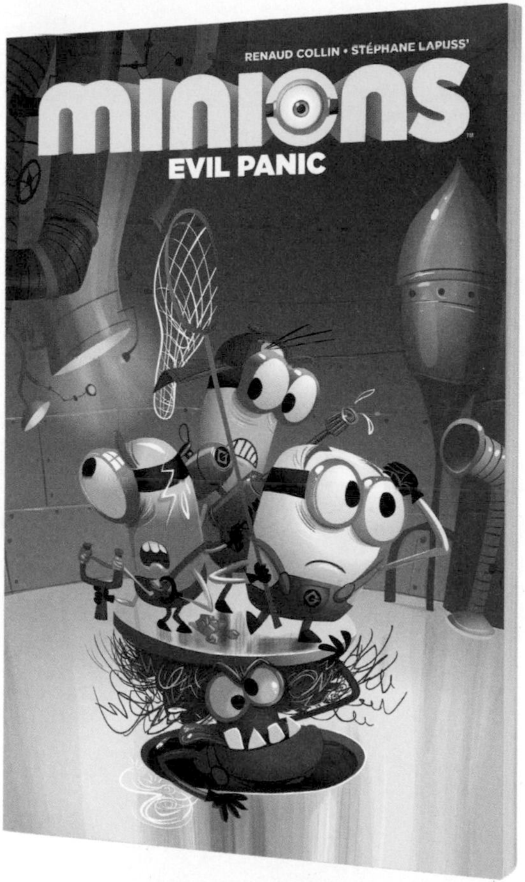
RENAUD COLLIN • STÉPHANE LAPUSS'
MINIONS
EVIL PANIC

## MINIONS VOL. 2: EVIL PANIC

While the villain Gru is busy taking over the world, his mischievious Minions embark on a journey of their own, fending off the evil Minions as they go about their work.

Softcover | $6.99 | £4.99
ISBN: 9781782765554
**OUT NOW**

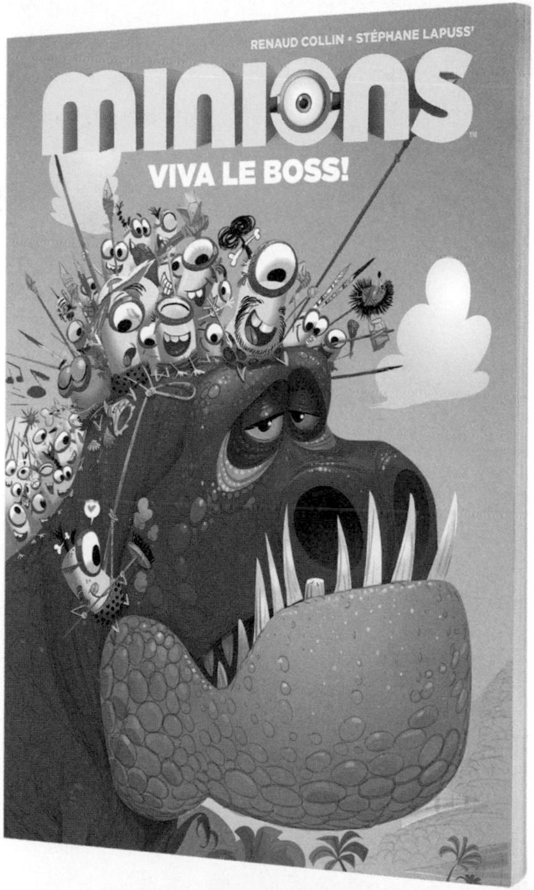
RENAUD COLLIN • STÉPHANE LAPUSS'
MINIONS
VIVA LE BOSS!

## MINIONS: VIVA LA BOSS

Hold on to your bananas - the Minions are back!
Back for more!
More chaotic catastrophes!
More astonishing journeys!

Softcover | $6.99 | £5.99
ISBN: 9781787730175
**OUT NOW**

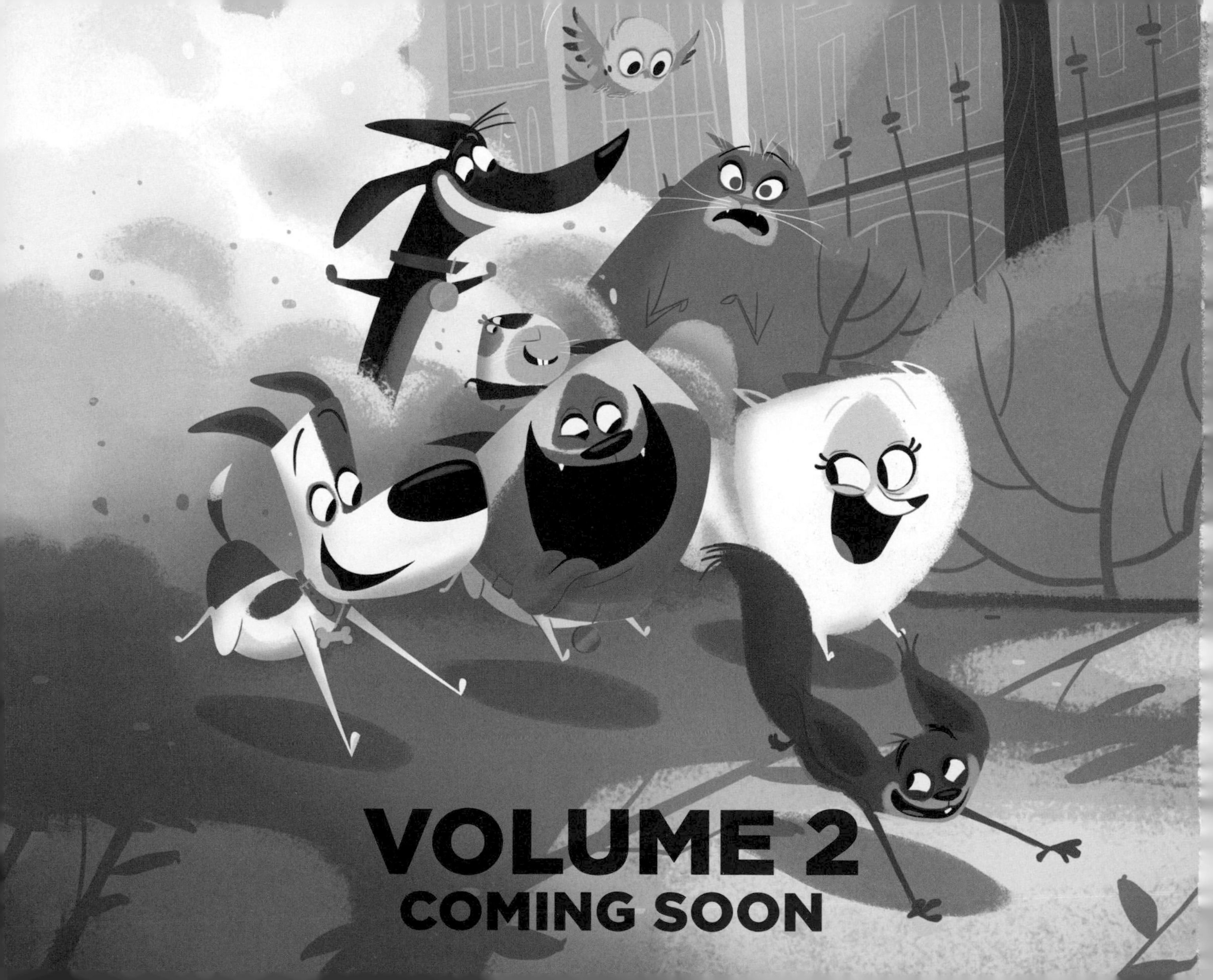
VOLUME 2
COMING SOON